More praise for
THE HOUSE IN THE WOODS

"The pace and natural dialogue keep the story moving."
BCCB

"Holland is on target when she's depicting Bridget's feelings of frustration about her looks and about her niche in the family, and there are plenty of readers who will identify with those problems."
Booklist

"Engrossing . . . Holland writes with skill."
The Kirkus Reviews

THE HOUSE IN THE WOODS

Isabelle Holland

FAWCETT JUNIPER • NEW YORK

RL1: $\dfrac{\text{VL } 5 \ \& \text{ up}}{\text{IL } 6 \ \& \text{ up}}$

A Fawcett Juniper Book
Published by Ballantine Books
Copyright © 1991 by Isabelle Holland

Library of Congress Catalog Card Number: 90-19834

ISBN 0-449-70410-6

This edition published by arrangement with Little, Brown & Company, Inc.

Manufactured in the United States of America

First Ballantine Books Edition: May 1992

THE HOUSE
IN THE WOODS

—1—

I found the house in the woods by accident, on a day when I thought I'd never find anything that would make my life better. And even though I was full of despair, the first sight, through the thick trees and matted vines, of the huge, decaying mansion, with its staring, empty windows, gave me a queer thrill. Although at that time I could not have said why.

We had never been to the lakeside before. Previous summer vacations had been spent on the Maine coast. But this year Daddy rented a cottage on a lake in northern New Hampshire.

When I asked him why we couldn't go back to our Maine island, he simply said, ''Maine is getting so crowded. Ingrid . . . Ingrid and I thought we ought to try something new. Morgan might do better here.''

''You might have asked me,'' I said indignantly. ''I've looked after Morgan more than Ingrid.''

''Well,'' Daddy asked impatiently, ''do you think Morgan was getting better—showing any signs of talking—where we used to go?''

The answer was no, and we both knew it. What I resented was his discussing it with Ingrid—Morgan's most recent baby-sitter–nanny—and not me. Ingrid had only come into our lives during the past few months. Since Mother had died five years ago, two years after

1

Morgan was born, I had looked after him. Of course there'd been baby-sitters and nannies, but they didn't feel about him the way I did, and he was always happier with me than with them.

When I said this to Daddy, right after he told me he'd hired this super-hotshot nanny type with special European training, his reply was, "Since he still can't talk, how do you know he prefers being with you?"

"I can tell," I said. "He has a special look on his face when he sees me."

"I've never even seen him smile," Daddy said, "so I'm bound to say I think you're imagining this. Yes, I know how you feel about him, and I think it's great. Sometimes—often—I wished you felt something approaching that for the twins."

I opened my mouth to say "the twins are boring." But I closed it without speaking.

There aren't many times lately I can forget that I'm adopted. Not that there's ever been any secret about it. Mother made a point of telling me as early as I can remember, saying always, in one way or another, "You see, we picked you, so you're special. When you have babies in the usual way, you have to take what you get!" And she'd grin in that wonderful way of hers and we'd both giggle.

So I never had any hesitation about saying the first thing that came to my mind, which often was tactless. Mother, if she was around, would tell me. "There goes Bridget again, with her tongue bumping into the furniture." Once before when I told her the twins were boring, she looked at me and smiled. "That's only because you're so nutty about Morgan—which is wonderful. One day you'll wake up and find Marian and Liza interesting. The trouble with you, Bridget, darling, is that you like problems, and the twins are—for the moment—problem-free. Just wait awhile! I can't imagine they

2

won't develop their own version of double, double, toil and trouble, sooner or later.''

And then, five years ago, when I was nine, the twins were five and Morgan was two, Mother died suddenly. Nothing was the same afterwards, except that I continued to adore Morgan and to find the twins boring.

When Ingrid came, two months before we left for the lake, one of her first comments to me was, ''Oh, your father tells me you're adopted. How interesting! I wonder where your parents came from!''

''Mother came from Boston, Daddy comes from Connecticut,'' I said, knowing perfectly well she wasn't talking about my adoptive parents.

''Oh—I know your father comes from New Haven.'' She showed lots of white teeth in a broad smile. ''I'm talking of your real parents.''

''These are my real parents,'' I said.

There was a short silence. Then I found an excuse to get out of the room.

From what I've read about adopted children, most of us wonder where our birth parents came from and sometimes struggle with feelings of abandonment by them. But I'd never really thought about it seriously, until the day Daddy brought home this tall, thin, athletic-looking blonde who looked about twenty-five and introduced her as Ingrid.

''We're very lucky to have Ingrid,'' Daddy said, introducing her. ''And I want you all to be especially helpful and good!''

I could see by Daddy's face that he admired her. He's tall and thin and fair-haired too, although his eyes are green, rather than blue.

''Hi!'' Marian and Liza said together, grinning broadly. With tow-colored straight hair and sea-blue eyes, they could have been Ingrid's children.

''Hi!'' Ingrid said, and grinned back. She turned to

3

Morgan, who had Mother's brown hair and gray eyes. I glanced down at him and knew he wasn't entirely happy with the situation. But Daddy was right, in a way. Morgan's expression didn't change and he didn't, of course, say anything. I knew how he felt, but I'd have had a hard time saying how I knew. Maybe it was something about the way his eyelids closed a little, or seemed to. And I could feel his hand touch mine.

"This must be Morgan," Ingrid said. She had an accent of some kind, although it was slight.

"Yes," I said. "This is Morgan."

She bent down. "I'm sure he would like to answer for himself." She paused. "Wouldn't you, Morgan?"

Daddy started, "I don't think—" The twins said bluntly, "But he can't." And Morgan shook his head violently and slid behind me a little.

Ingrid looked up at me. Then she drew slowly to her height and looked down at me. "And you're Bridget."

I nodded and then said, "Yes."

"The changeling," she said, still smiling.

"I'm not a changeling," I said angrily. "I'm adopted. Morgan and the twins aren't, but I am!"

"Ah, that must be why you look so different! With your black hair and being short."

"And fat," I finished defiantly. It had been a sore subject since I was nine.

"Oh no. Not fat. Pleasingly plump. But I'll help you with exercises. I used to work in a health club, you know!"

"You're certainly a walking advertisement for it," Daddy said with admiration.

"My goodness," she said. "Now, you mustn't spoil me."

"Will you help us, too?" the twins asked. They were both skinny. Somehow that made it worse.

"But you don't need it!"

4

I'd often read about people grinding their teeth, though I was never sure what it meant. Now I knew. I could feel my jaws locked together.

Ingrid said to me, "Your father tells me how bright you are, and what a dedicated reader!"

"Too much so," Daddy said, still looking enchanted. "I want her—and Morgan, too—to get out more this summer." He smiled. "Get a tan like yours."

"I don't tan," I said, and could hear how stubborn and uncooperative I sounded. "I turn red and then blister."

"I know just the tanning liquid for you. And you have to go at it slowly!"

"I hate lying out on a towel in the sun, doing nothing, except getting hotter and hotter. It's boring!"

"Maybe," Liza put in, "it's because you told me you don't really look good in a bathing suit."

"At the end of the summer," Ingrid said, "the boys will be lining up to ask you out!"

"You'd like that, Bridget, wouldn't you?" Daddy said. His eyes were on Ingrid.

"No," I said. "I think boys are boring."

"You think far too many things and people are boring," Daddy said.

"It's not important," Ingrid said. "We'll talk about it later."

To my vast relief, I felt Morgan's tug on my hand. I knew it meant he wanted to go somewhere. "We—Morgan and I—have to go," I said.

"Wouldn't you like to stay for a bit, while I teach you some interesting new games I learned last year?"

Morgan may be mute, but he can hear and understand perfectly well. I got a certain satisfaction out of seeing how violently he shook his head.

"All right, another time," Ingrid said.

"I'm sure you'd love to learn some new games,"

5

Daddy said, sounding a little stern. Morgan's inability to talk has always made him irritable. "I think it's because he doesn't understand what's stopping Morgan," Mother once said.

"Don't the doctors know?" I asked.

She sighed. "They can't seem to agree, though most of them say it's nothing physical." She paused. "They think he'll grow out of it. After all, he's only two, and as they keep telling me, boys are supposed to be slower about talking than girls."

"You mean, one day he'll just talk!"

"Something like that. If there was anything physical, I think your father would understand it better."

"But what will make him talk?"

"Honey, if I knew, if they knew, I could answer you. Right now they don't. But he's been examined so much and poked and looked at so much that I'm going to make sure he's left alone for at least a year."

But before that year had ended, Mother was dead.

Morgan still didn't talk. As the years passed and his silence continued, Daddy took him to a variety of doctors and specialists. After each siege Morgan would seem to retreat further into himself. Normally he ran around, played games and, except for speaking, took part. After he'd been to a group of doctors, he wouldn't do any of that. He just sat and read, or stared out the window. Then, slowly, he'd go back to being the way he was before. No one ever told me exactly what they thought was wrong with Morgan, but because they didn't seem to think it was physical, I assumed they thought it was psychological.

I knew one thing: Morgan hated to have people try to teach him or train him. "Now, just see if you can make this vowel sound, Morgan," one baby-sitter used to say. Morgan kept as far from her as he could.

When the time came that Morgan had to go to school,

6

Daddy talked to the local schools in our Connecticut town. There was one for "special children," but Morgan, who was taken there twice when he was six, hated it so much he refused to go back. It was true, of course, that he could have been picked up and carried there, but when that was tried, he seemed to disappear into a depression. So Daddy decided to postpone the whole thing for a year. As far as IQ tests and other tests were concerned, he came out as bright—but he still couldn't talk.

I could tell almost immediately that Daddy put great hopes in Ingrid, and I was fairly sure that Morgan knew that, too. So I was slightly amused when he did everything he could to avoid her.

During school, I wasn't there with the two of them, but I could see by the way Morgan came barreling out of the house when I got back that he couldn't wait to leave whatever they were doing.

I don't know what Ingrid said to Daddy. What she said to me was, "You seem to be fond of your little brother, and he certainly likes you. I'm surprised you haven't been able to help him more."

I had worried about that, too, for a while, but I knew, somehow, that one of the reasons he loved me was that I accepted him as he was; I didn't push him. Then I'd think I was being selfish.

Once I said to him, "Morgan, Ingrid thinks, and I guess a lot of people think, I should be helping you to learn how to talk. But I think you don't want me to. Is that true?"

He nodded so emphatically I thought he might knock his head off and said so. He just grinned.

And that's how things stood when we left for the lake.

The house Daddy had rented was white frame and a little way up a hill above Badger Lake. The woods that seemed to cover most of the area surrounding the lake had been thinned around the sides and back of the house. In front the property slanted gently down to a wide sandy beach. In back of the house was the road that led from the town of Jefferson, five miles to the east. On the other side of the road the woods grew thick up a hill, then down into a valley, and up again to another, higher hill. It was much more isolated and didn't seem as friendly as our place in Maine, where people were always on the street or the dock.

"How did you come to pick this place?" I asked Daddy as we carried the things from the car into the house.

"Somebody at the office told me about it," he said. "I know you think you would have preferred going to the old place, and we can always go back there next year, but it was getting filled with tourists and becoming rackety. Even during the week you could hardly go to sleep for all the noise. And I don't think all that noise and confusion was helping Morgan. Up here, in the peace and quiet, we can maybe help him some."

"You weren't there weeknights," I said.

"Look, if you don't like it here, it's not forever. Let's at least give it a try."

So we went in and unpacked. When I was through I went out onto the big screened porch and stared at the lake.

There were, I was glad to see, a few other houses at our end of the lake, although they weren't near. Boats of various kinds—rowboats, sailboats and even one motorboat—were visible on the water, and I suddenly knew why my father was attracted to the place. He loved sailing, although he never had much chance to do it, and had been thrilled last year to discover that the twins shared his enthusiasm. I didn't like it, and Morgan refused to go on a boat. The water around the Maine shore

8

had been too rough for a lot of sailing, but here it would be much better.

I stood there in the dusk, staring west. The scene was wild and beautiful. Everything seemed perfect for a wonderful holiday. But a weird sort of depression seemed to have settled on me. In a strange way I felt trapped.

— 2 —

Things didn't start out well.

Ingrid was an organizer. The morning after we arrived, she organized lying on the beach and, when I protested, produced a bottle of something that she swore would keep me from blistering and would give me a nice, even tan.

"I hate lying out there doing nothing," I said again.

"Didn't you tell me you had been given a reading list from school and if you read all the books, you might get into a special advanced class?"

I wished now I hadn't told her anything. "Yes," I said grudgingly.

"Well, then, you can start while you're getting a tan. I shall be there and I promise you I won't let you burn."

"Plenty of vitamin D in sun, Bridg," Daddy said. He was busy looking at a huge book on sailing.

"I take vitamin D, lots of it," I said.

"Much better to get it the natural way," Ingrid said. "Now, Liza, Marian, you're all fixed, are you? Did you remember to bring that big towel of yours?"

"And what about Morgan?" I asked. "He doesn't like to lie in the sun, either."

Ingrid hesitated, the first time I'd ever seen her do that.

Daddy said, "We've told Morgan that all the rest of

10

us will be sitting out there so he can come and play."
He paused. "He doesn't have to lie still. I know that's
hard for him." He added, "He can build sandcastles or
. . . or something."

"Come on, Bridg," Marian said. "You never know.
It might be fun."

Liza was staring over Daddy's shoulder at the book.
"Are we going to get a boat, Daddy?"

"We already have. It's going to be brought day after
tomorrow. Then we can take turns going out. I'm afraid
it's not big enough to carry all of us at the same time. I
thought it better to start small."

So an hour later, there I was, lying on the beach on
my towel, covered with some slippery goo, and wishing
I had put up more of a fight about coming to this place.
At least in Maine I knew some of the other kids, and
there was a street to stroll down and an ice cream parlor
to drop in to. But I pushed that out of my mind. Maybe
this was the summer I'd really get thinner.

We'd been there about an hour when suddenly from
down the beach came the sound of shouts and laughter.

We all sat up.

A bunch of boys and girls were pouring out of the
house nearest to us, which was still some distance away.
They put up some kind of a net and started throwing a
big ball back and forth.

Ingrid glanced at me. "Why don't you go down there
and see if you can join in?"

"No," I said. I didn't even have to think. For one
thing, they seemed a little older than me. For another,
they looked very tan, very athletic, and all the girls had
beautiful figures.

"I think it might be a good idea," Daddy said. He'd
turned over and was still reading his book.

Morgan was going on building his sandcastle, which
was almost finished. He'd brought up enough water from

11

the lake so that he'd been able to shape the damp sand into a fairly large, quite elaborate structure with four-square walls and something in the corners that could easily have been towers.

"That's terrific, Morgan," I said.

"They also have younger children," Ingrid said, still looking down the beach. "See, Morgan. There are two boys and a girl." And suddenly she got to her feet, picked up her towel, and waved.

I was sitting up and saw what happened then. The small children saw her and started running towards us. Then one of the volleyball players noticed Ingrid and must have said something to the others, because they started loping in our direction, too.

Morgan and I looked at each other. It's funny, we're not related by blood, but it's as though we were part of one another. I knew in that instant that both of us felt terribly uncomfortable—out of it, not part of this good-looking, athletic crowd. And then, as the first of the volleyball players jumped over the low string of rocks that divided the property, I also knew, almost as though I could see it, what was going to happen.

"Watch out for the sandcastle!" I yelled. But it was too late. The leading girl, right behind the leading boy, kicked it so the sand went flying. She probably didn't mean to. She was just following the boy.

I saw Morgan's face and got up.

"You kicked over his castle," I said angrily, the first words I spoke to our neighbors.

Her eyebrows went up. "Sorry, I didn't see it. I thought you wanted us to come over here."

"We do," Ingrid said enthusiastically.

Then Daddy was on his feet. "Of course we do. Thank you for coming over. Bridget!"

Ingrid pushed me towards the girl. "It was an accident, of course," Ingrid said brightly. "And Morgan

12

can always build another, can't you?" She flicked him on the cheek.

He stepped back. I ignored the girl and went over to him. "It was an accident, Morgan. We'll build another one together."

One of the boys said something and the group laughed.

"Can we play with you?" Liza asked. Then, "This is Marian, my twin sister."

The girl who had kicked Morgan's sandcastle said, "I'm Linda Martin. Sure, you and Marian can come and play." She turned towards Daddy and Ingrid. "Nice to have met you." To Morgan she said, "I'm sorry about your sandcastle." Then without looking at me she left, with her group and the twins running after her.

Daddy looked at me. "You could at least have shown a little courtesy."

"Bridget, you were not polite," Ingrid said. "You should go after her and apologize."

I felt Morgan's hand touch my arm.

"She shouldn't have kicked over Morgan's sandcastle." I knew I hadn't been polite. If Ingrid just hadn't put her oar in, I might have gone over and said I was sorry. But she had. "Morgan, let's build another one further up the beach where nobody'll run over it."

So for the next hour Morgan and I mixed sand with water and slowly constructed another castle as much like the first as we could.

By that time I was beginning to feel the slow burn on my skin and realized I hadn't been dousing myself with the stuff Ingrid had given me.

"Listen, Morgan," I said. "I'm going to have to go in. I'm beginning to feel the burn on my shoulders, and I don't want Ingrid to start going on about how I should have used the stuff she gave me."

He nodded.

I glanced back and saw Ingrid and Daddy looking at the sailing book together. The twins were busy tearing around the beach with the younger kids. Picking up my towel, I ran to the house. My book was still on the beach, but I hoped that the depressingly neat Ingrid would bring it in with her.

I took a shower, wincing under the drops that bounced on my shoulders, smeared all the cream I could lay hold of on my arms and back and then slid a soft T-shirt over that. Putting on my jeans, I wondered then what I was going to do next.

If we'd been at our old summer standby, I'd have strolled down the main street of the village, maybe dropped in to the ice cream parlor, where I'd have eaten a cone or two I didn't need, but I'd at least have been around some other kids and might have joined them on whatever project they'd go on to. Or I would have stopped in at the bookstore with Morgan, where I'd look into a whole bunch of mystery books, reading as much as I could, and he'd do the same with drawing and art books. Or I'd—

Suddenly it swept over me how isolated we were here. Why on earth didn't Daddy think about that when he decided to change our usual summer place?

I'll bet it's Ingrid, I thought angrily, and wondered what was in it for her to bring us here. Why didn't my father think more about what was good for us, about what we did and needed to do during the summer, instead of just himself? And I never knew he was interested in sailing because he never said he was.

At that moment he and Ingrid came in.

"Let me look at your shoulders," Ingrid said. "I hope you kept putting that cream on I gave you."

I moved off. "My shoulders are fine. Daddy, why couldn't you have sailed off the coast where we were last summer?"

14

"I've told you several times, Bridget, that I didn't think that place was good for Morgan. He never improved, never showed any signs of talking there."

"Well, he didn't during the winter, either."

Daddy started to look cross.

Ingrid glanced at him and said, "We felt that here, by ourselves, we might have a better chance of teaching him to talk. From the way your father described it, you were all so busy running around, you hardly had time for him."

"That's not true! I used to take him with me lots of times," I said.

"And it didn't do any good, did it? He still isn't talking. Together, here, we can all help him."

"He was doing very well with play therapy at the family therapy place."

"How do you know?" Daddy said. "He still didn't say anything."

"But the therapist said he was beginning to show definite patterns in the figures he picked up."

"Figures?" Dad interrupted.

"You know—family play figures. Only the end of school came and we had to come here."

"If you want to spend the summer in the hot city—" Ingrid said.

"No, but we could have gone to our usual place, and I don't think it would have been any different for Morgan."

"Only *you* would have had a better time." Daddy's voice was cold. "You're being very selfish, Bridget. We came here so we could all be together and pay attention to Morgan. Personally, I don't have much faith in all this play therapy nonsense. I think Morgan just needs to make an effort. There's probably some . . . some physical thing that the doctors overlooked. As we all have reason to know, they're far from infallible."

15

"But they said we're not to bug him, that whatever was blocking him would just close up tighter than ever if we nag him or try to make him say words. And he does close up. I see it, when you start trying to make him talk. And I don't think it's fair for you to call me selfish. It's my vacation, too."

"Sorry you don't want to help Morgan," Daddy said, in a closed-off voice.

"But I do—"

Daddy turned his back and started talking to Ingrid. It's something he's always done when he's angry with me. I knew he didn't think much of the family therapy foundation that—reluctantly—he'd taken Morgan to. He doesn't think much of therapy of any kind, and if it had been anybody but Morgan, he'd have dug in his heels. But up till that time nothing had worked, and the child therapists and counselors thought it was a good idea. All the doctors who had examined Morgan had told Daddy again and again that there was nothing physically wrong with Morgan. His hearing was perfect. But after Mother's death, Daddy became disillusioned about the medical profession as a whole. Nobody had really found out what was wrong with Mother until it was too late. So he became bitter about doctors. "They're in it for the money and the glory," he often said. He liked psychiatry and therapy even less. "A bunch of incompetent, dependent people going and crying on somebody's shoulder for a hundred and twenty-five an hour," he once said to me.

"It helps some people," I had replied at the time.

"So does telling their fortune with tea leaves," he snapped back.

At that point Morgan entered the room and came over to where I stood.

"Bridget, come into the kitchen and help me fix lunch," Ingrid said. "The twins'll be down in a minute and they'll pitch in, too. Morgan, why don't you relax with your father."

Morgan looked from me to Daddy.

"That's right, Morgan. Come over here and we'll read the paper together," Daddy said.

Morgan threw me a glance. I winked at him and shrugged my shoulders.

Twenty minutes later Ingrid and I were setting the table in the breakfast-dining room. She'd made a huge salad and put whole wheat rolls on the table. The twins and Morgan had milk, she and Daddy had coffee. When she asked me what I wanted, I said coffee.

"You're too young for coffee," she said. "When you're sixteen you can have it, if you still want it."

"All right, then, a Coke."

"That's fattening and has caffeine."

"A Diet Coke."

"That's—"

"Either you let me have a Diet Coke or I start walking to town where I can get one."

"That's at least five miles!"

"So can I have my Diet Coke?"

She sighed. "Very well, but I don't think it's a good idea for somebody with a weight problem to get into the diet soda habit. If you only knew what chemicals you're drinking! Just plain water or skim milk would be far better."

I had vaguely thought of skim milk, even though I hate it. But at that point it was Diet Coke or revolution. "I want a Diet Coke."

When I came back to the breakfast room with my Coke, Morgan was standing by the window watching a bird peck on the small lawn at the back. Daddy, his mouth rather set, was sitting down at the table.

"How did the reading go?" Ingrid asked cheerfully.

"All right," Daddy said.

Morgan came over, took me by the hand, dragged me back to the window and pointed at the birds.

"Those are sea gulls and . . . and finches, I think," I said, "but I'm not sure about the finches."

At that moment the twins ran in. "Can we have lunch with the Burroughses? They've invited us. But Mrs. Burroughs said we had to come back here to ask."

"Quite right," Ingrid said. She glanced towards Daddy.

"I think you'd better stay here for our first lunch," he said. "I'm sure they'll ask you again."

Ingrid started serving the salad. "I'll be going into town around four-thirty. But I thought we'd all get together and play a game after lunch. Liza, why don't you go and call Mrs. Burroughs and thank her, but tell her we want you to stay here just on the first day."

Liza, looking sulky, went out of the dining room. Marian sat down next to Daddy. Opposite him on the other side of the round table, Ingrid was still serving the salad.

"What kind of a game?" Liza asked, coming back into the room and sitting down at the table.

Ingrid smiled. "Just an easy game we all can play. We deal out some cards and then each person tries to guess what cards everybody else has in his or her hand."

It was such an obvious ploy to get Morgan to talk! I glanced at him. His face had that still, closed-in look it sometimes wore. I knew it meant he didn't want to be bothered or badgered. I opened my mouth, caught my father's look and then closed it again. It was no use arguing with Ingrid, and it was also no use now putting up a fight for the kind of play therapy Morgan had been doing. It looked pretty unlikely that there'd be anything like that up here, and, for the moment, we were stuck. I glanced again at Morgan. He was staring down at his plate. I remembered suddenly that he did not like salad.

18

I also remembered that he loved peanut butter. Jumping up, I went into the kitchen, got some butter out of the refrigerator, and searched the cupboard for some peanut butter. There wasn't any.

Going back, I said, "There's no peanut butter."

"I know," Ingrid said. "I'll get some this afternoon. Morgan, you can eat your salad —"

That was as far as she got before Morgan picked up his bowl of salad and threw it on the floor.

— 3 —

There was a moment's silence, then Liza gasped and Marian giggled. Daddy jumped up and Ingrid said sternly, "Morgan! That is very naughty. It's not acceptable behavior at all. Now I want you—"

Daddy had gone over to Morgan. "You're going to pick up every piece! Do you hear me? I know you're not deaf—"

"Daddy!" I went over to Morgan. "Look, I'll help you. Come on, let's start picking up."

But Morgan pushed me away and ran out the front door.

"Morgan!" I called after him, then went in pursuit. But Daddy, who besides being tall is quite athletic, passed me with no trouble and had caught up with Morgan before he reached the gate in the fence that surrounded the house.

He grasped Morgan's shoulders and tried to turn him around. "You're going to come back into the house and pick up what you threw on the floor. I know you have problems, but there's no reason you can't behave."

Morgan struggled against his hands and almost wriggled free. With that, Daddy picked up Morgan and started back towards the house. I could see Morgan's legs thrashing violently.

I called across to him, "Daddy, he hates to be picked up like that. I'll bring him back in."

"He has to learn that some behavior is just not tolerable. The fact that he is . . . that he's . . . that he doesn't talk doesn't change that."

Poor Daddy! Part of me raged against him for the way he was acting towards Morgan. But I also knew that he couldn't bring himself to admit that Morgan, his only son, was technically handicapped. It was easier for him to think Morgan was simply not trying hard enough.

He stalked back to the house with Morgan struggling harder in his arms with every step.

Part of me wanted to say, Put him down, I'll bring him in. But another part didn't want Morgan to think I was siding with Daddy. So I followed. I was also afraid of what might happen when Morgan, feeling helpless, went into a rage.

"Now," Daddy said, putting Morgan down beside the table, "Ingrid has picked up some of the salad, but you're going to pick up the rest. When you make a mess, you have to clean it up."

But what I'd been fearing exploded. Morgan lay down on the floor and started screaming and kicking, thrashing his legs and arms.

He hadn't done this since Ingrid had been with us. In fact, he hadn't done it for a long time. She stared. "Is he having a seizure?" she asked anxiously.

I knew he wasn't, but I waited for Daddy to answer. But he had gone white and was just staring.

"Come on, Morgan," I said and went over to him. I knelt down and added quietly, near his ear, "Stop yelling. Do you want to be tied down?"

I knew he feared that more than anything, not, of course, because he'd told me, but because one of his previous baby-sitters had tried it and he'd gone ber-

21

serk—bitten her and banged his head against the floor so violently he almost injured himself.

"Now get up," I said. I was worried that Daddy might decide Morgan should go to an institution. It had come up once or twice, and I knew it could be there in the back of Daddy's mind. I again leaned over Morgan and whispered into his ear so the others couldn't hear, "Do you want to be sent away?"

He slowed the thrashing, then stopped. I stood up and said in a normal voice, "Come on, Morgan, get up! I'll help you with the salad."

"No!" Daddy almost snapped. "Morgan must pick it up. I'd expect you or Liza or Marian to do the same and I don't see why Morgan should be different."

"Do it, Morgan," I said, "and get it over with."

But he saw his chance and ran out the front door and across the road. A car coming along just missed him. He scrambled up the bank on the other side and disappeared among the trees.

"I'm going to put a stop to this," Daddy said, striding towards the door.

"Daddy, please, let me go! I can get him back. You're going about it the wrong way. Please!"

"I don't see—"

"Yes," Ingrid said, surprising me. "It is better if Bridget goes. You can talk to him when he's back here and is calmed down." As Daddy hesitated, she repeated, "It is better if Bridget goes."

His face remained hard for a moment, and then suddenly changed. He seemed almost bewildered. My mother's words, spoken years back, went through my mind: "Your father is wonderful with figures and scientific calculation and computers. He's considered a whiz by a lot of experts in his field. But Bridget, he's not a people person." I remembered her hand on my face. "Darling, try to remember, he never means to be

22

unkind. He has a strong sense of justice, but it's in the abstract. And I'm not sure he's going to change.''

What was going on at that minute to make her say that? I couldn't remember. It didn't matter now. But she was right. And he had not changed.

''All right,'' he said, turning to me. ''But I want you to get across to him that he cannot behave this way. I don't understand why—'' He stopped there.

Teachers, doctors and psychologists had talked to him about the shock and trauma of Mother's death and the kind of therapy that might bring it out into the open and remove whatever was blocking his speech. But for reasons I never really understood, my father didn't or wouldn't hear them. Once I heard him mutter, ''Primitive tribes have witch doctors. I guess psychiatry is our version.''

I ran on out after Morgan, crossed the road and went up the bank. Then I stopped and looked around to see if I could find any clue as to where he might have gone. The trees grew close to the bank and fairly thickly in back of it. There were no footprints, but there was the bare trace of a path that seemed to zigzag between the trees. I started walking quickly on that.

I'm not sure how long I walked, but after what seemed like only a few minutes I was well out of sight of the road and the cottage. The trees here were an odd mixture of pines and other kinds—sycamore, chestnut, oak and some others I wasn't able to identify. I thought about calling Morgan's name, but I was afraid that in his present state of mind he would run from any voice, even mine.

Then I saw him sitting cross-legged under a big oak off to one side a good distance from the path. He was placing small stones in what looked vaguely like a circle.

''Hi!'' I said to him, going over.

He looked up and I could see he had been crying.

Sitting down beside him, I put my arm around him. "It's going to be okay, Morgan," I said. "Honestly!" I really didn't know whether it was or not, but when I let myself believe it wasn't, either for him or me, the despair was awful.

When Daddy was severe, the first thing Mother had always said to me was, "You know your father loves you." I knew why she said it, so I wouldn't think he didn't. But it was hard to believe her when he had just finished scolding me for a poor grade or eating an extra potato. She wanted to reassure me—and perhaps herself, I thought later, when I was older—that he did indeed love me. But I wasn't reassured. For me, love was being kissed and encouraged and praised. It wasn't just a feeling that didn't show in any outward sign. If I couldn't feel it, it didn't exist. So I didn't repeat Mother's words now to Morgan. I just sat there. I couldn't really know what was going on inside of him, though I could feel his misery and fear.

We'd been sitting there for a while when I thought I heard a tiny sound. I looked up and found myself staring into a pair of golden eyes in the face of a cat.

It was a ginger cat, with striped markings of a lighter and darker cinnamon color, and a white front. Its ears were forward, one paw upraised. I'd always loved animals. We'd had a big retriever before Mother died, but it was killed in an accident and after that Daddy said he preferred to wait until we were older. Dogs needed walking and looking after, something baby-sitters didn't like to do, and he didn't care for cats.

"Cat!" I said, springing up.

It was the wrong thing to do. With a curious sound, the cat turned and started running deep into the trees. Without even thinking, I went after it and could hear Morgan's steps following me.

24

But of course the cat was far swifter than we were. For a while as we ran, we could catch a glimpse of it as it sped among the trees, sometimes almost invisible in the undergrowth and bushes. And then we lost it altogether.

We stood there then, staring through the trees. The sun didn't penetrate much here, so we were surrounded by a twilit dusk, even though outside it was the middle of the afternoon. It was very quiet. The wind blew softly among the leaves and then, for a while, stopped. Everything was silent. I kept staring in the direction that the cat had been going when I last looked, but I knew it didn't mean anything. It could have veered off anywhere.

Slowly I started turning in a half circle, thinking perhaps I'd see the cat if I was careful not to let my feet make any noise against leaves or branches. But there was no lightning strip of orange that had kept me in pursuit before. As I was about to turn around and look for our path, though, I saw something else. At first I thought it was an odd collection of shadows, curtains formed by the combination of leaves and shafts of sunlight that came through the trees. Then, suddenly, I felt a motion beside me. Morgan, who had been running with me and was now standing next to me, took my hand and with the other arm pointed.

"It's a house," I said to Morgan, and my voice sounded like an intrusion. The house looked so old it was like something out of a fairy tale.

Morgan started pulling me towards it.

"I'll bet the cat's there," I said. "If I were a wild cat, that would be just the place I'd take over."

Morgan and I walked forward, picking our way among the bushes, stepping over fallen branches. Finally the house reared up in front of us. A queer feeling went through me. It wasn't fear. It was more like a sudden wild hope. But for what I didn't know; it made no sense.

The house seemed enormous. All the windows had arches above the panes, angled like elbows, and there were gabled windows in the roof.

The glass in the windows on the first floor was broken here and there, and pieces of cardboard or paper had been put in the holes. Some of the windows above were intact. They were all filthy. The steps leading to a sort of veranda were broken. As we moved slowly forward there was a sound of creatures scurrying away out of our path.

Finally we reached the edge of the veranda.

"I don't think we ought to trust those steps," I said.

Morgan, who could be athletic when he was so minded, jumped up and then held out his hand to me.

"Thanks." I put a sneakered foot on the rickety porch and got up on it. For a moment I thought the entire porch shook, and I wondered what it would bring down if it finally broke. But after a little creaking and swaying, it held. Morgan and I walked over to the front door. It had once been red. I could see streaks of scarlet under the dust and dirt. There was a knob, but it was hanging out. So I pushed against the door and it swung open.

Cat, who was across the room in front of an empty fireplace, suddenly looked up. Beneath her were what looked like soft dark and light orange balls; then one of them moved and I could see they were kittens. Besides the orange kittens, there were two black and one multicolored.

On the other side of the empty hearth a light blazed down on a slanted table. Seated at the table was a woman, her hand poised, holding something slender. She was looking at us.

"Come in," she said. "I've been expecting you."

—4—

Slowly we walked forward. I could feel Morgan's hand gripping mine.

"Why—why were you expecting us?" I asked. "We've only just discovered this house."

"Because Tiger came running back and said you were on your way."

When I looked puzzled, she pointed what I now saw was a paintbrush towards our guide. "Meet Tiger," she said. "Tiger, meet—" She glanced at me.

"Bridget. And this is Morgan."

"Hello, Bridget. Hello, Morgan." When she looked at Morgan I said, "Morgan doesn't talk."

"How sensible of him!"

Suddenly Morgan grinned. She didn't, I decided, sound like anybody else I'd known.

"What are you painting?"

"Illustrations for fairy stories."

"Can I look?"

"Yes. But not too often. You can come over here and look now if you want. I've been trying to think of somebody I could use as a model for my current heroine, and I think you might be just right."

I heard my own voice come out. "I'm too fat!"

She sighed. "Somebody must have told you that. I wonder why people rush around telling other people

27

how they ought to behave and ought to look. You have a pretty face and I expect you're the right size for you at this point in your life.''

For some reason I could feel tears in my eyes and was instantly ashamed. I looked down at my feet and tried to keep my eyelids as wide apart as possible so they wouldn't overflow.

Then, to my astonishment, I could see Morgan walk across to her, take her hand and nod his head vigorously.

''I'm glad you agree with me, Morgan. You are plainly very wise.''

She moved her feet and I could see her long wide skirt flowing over the floor. She was young, although not as young as Ingrid—maybe in her thirties—with brown hair and light brown eyes. She wasn't exactly pretty, but I liked her face.

''You're probably thinking that it's crazy for anyone to come here wearing a skirt like this,'' she said, ''so I'll tell you right away I don't. I keep the skirt here to work in. I feel far more comfortable in it than I do in jeans or pants—certainly when I paint.''

Morgan started to walk over to the cat and her kittens.

''Morgan, go very quietly and slowly,'' the woman said. ''Tiger has had, I think, a rather hard life and is suspicious of anybody she doesn't know, especially where her kittens are concerned.''

It was obviously true. Tiger was now crouched, braced against the floor, her yellow eyes on Morgan, her tail swishing back and forth. The kittens, mewing around one another, had such round heads that their ears barely showed and their eyes were all closed.

''Just stay quite still and hold out your finger like this,'' the woman said. And putting down the paintbrush, she held out her hand with one finger extended.

"If she doesn't feel you're a threat to her kittens—or her—she won't take offense."

So Morgan stood there for a minute, his finger out, and then, moving gently, he squatted down, still holding out his hand and finger. I could see Tiger suddenly tense as Morgan bent his knees, but after a while she straightened her legs a little and slowly, very slowly, walked towards him.

Morgan didn't move, just continued holding out his finger. Tiger smelled his finger for a while, then tentatively rubbed her head against it, then against his hand, and after that against his leg.

He patted and stroked her head and back.

"I haven't seen her do that before," the woman said. "But then, to be truthful, I haven't seen her with anyone else. She didn't do that with me right away."

"Do you live here?" I asked.

She grinned suddenly. "No. Not hardly. I come here when I can, and I keep my skirt and painting blouse here, but I don't think it would be a . . . well, a good place to live."

"Why not?" For some strange reason I wanted to contradict her. I wanted very much for her to say that living here would be wonderful.

Instead, she looked at me for a moment and then said, "Have you been here before?"

"No. I told you. Morgan and I followed Tiger here. We haven't been here before."

She didn't say anything so I said again, "Why don't you think it would be a good place to live?"

"Well, for one thing, I'm not sure how well the plumbing works. I haven't had to try it too often. But when I did, the first time it flooded and the next time it didn't work at all. So now—when needs must, I go outside."

Morgan had been letting Tiger smell him and rub

29

against him, but at that moment he stood up. Tiger sprang back with a hiss and tore over to her kittens. Morgan started after her, but she turned and spat.

His face, which had been happy and peaceful, looked upset. He glanced at me.

"The best thing is not to make any sudden moves," the woman said. "Just remember, until very recently all humans to her have been The Enemy." Her voice put capitals on the words.

I started looking around. It was a big room with high ceilings. Paper hung in strips from the walls and what didn't hang down was covered with dirt except for lighter square and rectangular patches on the walls.

"Were pictures in the paler spaces?" I asked.

"I imagine so."

There wasn't much furniture: a sofa with the stuffing out, a couple of straight chairs, an old scratched table. The floor had a beat-up carpet on it, with holes and areas where the weaving showed. Curtains hung crazily from broken rods.

I glanced at Morgan. He had apparently reestablished some kind of relationship with Tiger and was sitting cross-legged about three feet away from her. The kittens tumbled around her, mewing and squeaking noisily. Then she lay down and like fuzzy soldiers they lined up at the milk bar.

"Dinner is served," the woman said.

She had said I could look at her painting, so I went around and stared over her shoulder. It was like looking at magic. There were trees and little creatures with funny hats which I took to be gnomes and small animals arranged in a circle.

"What are they doing?"

"They're considering whether to go on a journey," she said.

There were a mouse, a larger mouse or rat, a cat, a

30

very small horse, two rabbits, a gerbil and what looked like two woodchucks, one large and one small. The gnomes were in back of them, watching them from behind bushes and trees, and in amongst the trees was something.

"What's between the trees?"

"A monster."

"What kind of a monster?"

"I'll show you when I've finished."

"What's the book about?"

"About a journey and a monster."

"Are you writing it?"

"No."

"Who is?"

There was a silence. Then the woman said, "Have you ever come across a poem that begins, ' "You are old, Father William," the young man said'?"

"Yes. *Alice in Wonderland.* It and *Through the Looking Glass* are two of my favorite books. Why?"

"Do you know how it ends?"

I tried to think, but nothing would come. "No."

She looked at me and smiled a little. " ' "I have answered three questions, and that is enough" '—"

"You mean you're tired of answering questions?"

"Yes. For the moment. But I would like to do a sketch of the next drawing using you as a model. Could you stand over there for a minute or so?" And she pointed to where she wanted me to stand.

I didn't like being told I shouldn't ask any more questions. It reminded me of Ingrid or Daddy, or both. Still, I did enjoy the idea of her using me as a model—that is, with certain provisions. "Make me thinner," I said. And added, "Please."

"I'll draw you as I see you," she said. "How's that?"

"All right," I said, but then thought, suppose she

31

sees me the way Ingrid does and Daddy sometimes does? Too fat. But she hadn't liked it when I'd said that.

So I stood where she indicated as she picked something up and started using it as a pencil. "Is that a pencil?" I asked.

"No, charcoal."

I was about to ask why she used it when I remembered the poem. So I closed my mouth and said nothing.

"All right," she said after a few minutes. "That's all I need right now. I'll do your face later."

"Can I see?" I burst out.

"No, not now. Later."

Still a little irritated, I began strolling around the room and then noticed what I hadn't seen before, a staircase going up to another floor. Again, I was about to ask where it led but swallowed my words. If she didn't want me to ask questions, I wouldn't talk.

I put a foot on the bottom stair. A loud creak sounded and I felt the whole structure move a little.

"I'd be careful if I were you. I went upstairs and nothing terrible happened, but I don't think any part of that is too secure. You'd better walk up on the side nearest the wall."

The staircase went up one wall, with the remains of paneling and what looked like wooden props on the outside.

Clinging to the inside of the stairs, I went slowly up. The creaking and the moving went on, but nothing else happened and I finally arrived at the upper floor. The stairs ended in a square hall, a smaller version of the one downstairs, with rooms opening off.

I stood there for a moment on the top step. For some reason I had a weird reluctance to go on and look at the upper floor. And the longer I stood, the more the reluctance grew. Even with all the dirt and missing furniture downstairs, there was something about it that made me feel—what? The word that kept pushing itself to the top of my mind was *happy*. Here the feeling was not happy. I felt increasingly uncomfortable.

"Don't be stupid," I said aloud.

There was a skittering of feet and something whizzed by my head, making the air quiver. I wanted to turn around and run down but couldn't move. It was as though I didn't have any legs or were paralyzed.

Suddenly the woman's voice floated up. "Are you all right?"

I opened my mouth but at first nothing came out.

"Bridget!"

"Yes," I could finally call back. "I'm okay." I'll look around another time, I thought, and knew I was just making excuses.

I heard a noise from downstairs and saw the woman push the table away, reach for something and then stand. I realized then that what she had reached for was a cane. "Bridget, come along down. I told you it wasn't too secure a place."

If she hadn't said that, I would have come down immediately. But I didn't want to give in to whatever was making me want to get away.

"I'm all right," I said, and took a step forward. And then another step and another. I had to force my feet to slide forward, one after the other.

What happened then I don't know. But the next thing I knew I was running down the stairs as quickly as I could, not even bothering with the banister.

"Come here, let me look at you," she said.

I ignored her. "Morgan," I said, "we have to go. Now."

He looked up at me from where he was sitting beside the kittens, his face puzzled. He shook his head.

"Yes," I said. "We have to. They'll be looking for

33

us.'' And I went over, reached down to his hand and tried to pull him up. But he snatched his hand away. It was obvious he wanted to play with the kittens.

"Maybe you'd better go, Morgan," the woman said. "You can come another time."

Finally he got up. I took him by the hand and almost ran him out of the house, down the rickety veranda steps and through the trees. I didn't even know where I was going. After a while I stopped in my tracks. What had happened to me? What had I felt? I didn't know. I couldn't remember. It was as though none of it had happened at all.

Morgan was standing there, looking at me.

"I'm sorry, Morgan. I don't know what got into me. But we'd better head home."

Somehow we had no trouble finding our way back. It had been so hard and bewildering getting there, but the return was as though a clear path existed, which it didn't.

When I saw the road and then, past the fence, the roof of the house we were in for the summer, I suddenly realized I hadn't asked the woman's name. I had no idea who she was.

—5—

When we reached the gate in the fence, Morgan stopped. Since his hand was in mine, that meant I stopped.

"What now?" I asked, trying to be gentle, because his face was troubled.

Suddenly he raised the other hand and made the gesture of throwing something on the floor.

I had forgotten about the salad. I had no idea how long we had been gone, but unless someone had defied Daddy, the various bits of salad would still be on the floor. Nothing quite like this had happened before, though in years past Morgan had certainly gone into rages.

"We're just going to have to face the music," I said. "We can't stay away forever." Just for a moment, I found myself wishing we could. It shocked me, because I had always assumed I loved Daddy, even though I knew he wasn't like Mother and sometimes had a hard time understanding things.

Morgan was looking up at me. "Would you rather go and try building a sandcastle?" I said.

He nodded vigorously, but at that moment the matter was resolved. Liza and Marian came bursting out of the house.

35

"Daddy and Ingrid have been looking for you," Liza said.

"They're worried," Marian said.

"And mad," Liza added. "They wanted to go out on the beach this afternoon and get some more sun. Now it's practically time for dinner."

"It can't be," I said sharply.

"It is," the twins said together. "It's almost five o'clock."

I couldn't believe we had been out that long. We'd sat down to lunch around one. The salad episode must have occurred about one-fifteen. Which meant we had been gone almost four hours.

"Where have you been?" Liza asked.

"We even went to the next cottage down the beach to find out if you were there. Ingrid said she was going to call the police," Marian said.

"Yes," Ingrid said, coming through the front door behind Liza, "I was going to give you another half hour and then call the police. It was very, very wrong of you, Bridget, to stay out like that. Very irresponsible. Your father is upset, and I don't blame him."

At that moment, like something out of a TV movie, Daddy arrived through the door.

"Where have you been?" he said.

My heart sank. Daddy never shouted when he was angry, his voice seemed to get quieter, but there was a note in it that scared the wits out of me. I could feel Morgan gripping my hand.

"We went for a walk in—" I could feel myself refusing to mention the house or the woods. I didn't want Daddy or Ingrid to know about either.

"Just where did you go?" Daddy's voice was still deadly quiet. His face had a white, set look that always meant he was furious.

I'm not a good liar. I stammer and stutter when I lie,

36

and I also do it when I'm flustered. "I—I—" And then as I looked frantically over the rolling fields leading down to the beach and the little woods that grew nearer the water further down, away from the neighbors, I said, "We went for a walk in those woods. They're nice." And I prayed hard that he didn't know anything about them.

"Didn't you hear us calling you?" Ingrid asked.

"No. We didn't. Did you, Morgan?" And I looked down at him, which gave me a chance to think.

He shook his head.

"I don't hold Morgan responsible," Daddy said. "But I do hold you, and I think you behaved with total disregard for anyone else, taking off like that."

He paused, and I waited, feeling a little sick. Often when he was angry he would hand out some punishment, and I dreaded what he would do up here.

"I won't punish you severely this time," he said finally. "But if you ever do this kind of thing again—wandering off by yourselves—I'm going to ground you. Is that understood?"

"Yes," I said, almost giddy with relief. I knew I was going back to the house in the woods. I knew I would not mention it to Daddy or Ingrid and would do anything to keep them from knowing. How I'd manage to do both I didn't know. But I'd find a way, somehow. In the meantime—for now, at least—the axe hadn't fallen.

I spent that night tossing and turning, trying to think of a way to go back to the house without being caught. As I did, I realized fully for the first time how well Daddy and Ingrid had managed to make it impossible for either Morgan or me to get away or be by ourselves. And I saw, for the first time, that it was probably deliberate. At our former summer place we were in and out all the time—mostly out. There were streets and stores

37

and the shore and ice cream and pizza parlors, all within a short walking distance. Daddy and I were never close. Sometimes it was hard for me to believe that both he and Mother wanted to adopt me. I had become pretty sure it was Mother who was the moving spirit behind that. And as long as she lived, he went along with it. After she died—well, he had the twins by then, and Morgan, although as far as liking to have him around, Morgan didn't count. He always got along well with Liza and Marian, but not with me and not with Morgan. So why was he so dead set on having us up here where he could keep an eye on us all the time?

As I turned in bed for the umpteenth time, flipping over my pillow and pounding it, I decided that it must be Ingrid's doing. Ingrid was an organizer, and he liked organization. And, of course, there was the boat. The thought of the boat, with us all squashed together in a space not a third of our living room, was so depressing I got up and went downstairs.

Eating in the middle of the night is the last thing I ought to do, and I knew it, but I couldn't cope with all the prohibitions surrounding me: no running outside and disappearing (besides, other than the house Morgan and I found, there was nowhere to run to), no extra eating, no going into town (not that I could, it would be a five-mile walk there and another five miles back). How could Daddy have been so unkind and so . . . so stupid! I stared at the refrigerator door.

"He's not stupid, darling, and you really mustn't say that!"

It was Mother's voice in my head, and it went on in words she'd often used, just as though she were there. "He's just—well, not very perceptive about people. He invents computer programs that work perfectly because they are set to absolute mathematical rules and which, once you understand them, are totally predictable!" And then in my head I heard her laugh and it was almost as though she were there putting her arms around me.

I opened the refrigerator door and was staring at the freezer section when I heard a slight noise behind me. I whirled around. Morgan was standing there.

"You ought to be asleep," I said.

He pointed to me.

"Yes, I ought to, too."

He came and stood beside me, staring at the refrigerator shelves.

"All right," I whispered. "We'll both have peanut butter sandwiches. But we'll have to be very quiet!"

He nodded.

Five minutes later we each had a peanut butter and jelly sandwich on a plate and a glass of milk to take upstairs. To stay downstairs would be asking for trouble. But there was the matter of washing the knife I'd used. I'd already discovered that turning on the water made a noise that went through the pipes all over the house. After a moment's thought I wrapped the knife in a paper napkin and put it on my plate. The peanut butter and jelly jars went back into the kitchen closets.

We were on the bottom step of the stairs when I heard Daddy's door open. We froze, and, very quietly, on my naked feet, I stepped back onto the floor and crouched down, so that my body couldn't be seen from the hall above. The long white T-shirt I was wearing as a night-gown would, I was sure, be all too visible. I could feel Morgan's small, skinny frame crouching behind me.

We stayed there, almost not breathing, while Daddy went to the bathroom.

I turned and whispered in Morgan's ear, "Did you close your door?" and then put my hand on his head so I could feel him shake or nod it. To my vast relief he nodded.

We stayed there until Daddy had returned to his bedroom and an extra few minutes more in case Ingrid should have been awakened and would come out of her room. But everything was quiet.

Morgan came into my room with me, since it was the farthest away from the two adults' rooms. Very quietly we ate our sandwiches and drank our glasses of milk. I hadn't put any light on, because it would shine under the door, but it wasn't really dark, because I had the blinds up and the moon and the stars were bright.

"You ready to go to your room now?" I whispered to Morgan, expecting to see him nod. But he didn't. He pointed to my bed. He sometimes liked to sleep with me and until now nobody minded. But once when Ingrid caught him going into my room and sliding into my bed, she was very firm that we were both too old for that.

I paused. Busily planning one act of rebellion—going to the old house—I wasn't anxious to get nailed for another. But something about Morgan's expression made me nod. "All right. But I'm going to push you out around six. If Ingrid looks in, you know what a fuss she'll make!"

Luckily the bed was pretty big, at least a double, if not bigger. I got into one side and he got in the other. Just before I went off to sleep I felt his back slide up against mine and heard a sigh as Morgan relaxed.

I always wake up early, so I was able to make Morgan get up and go to his own room as quietly as possible.' When I saw him close his door, I went back to bed for a nap. But instead I lay there, trying to think of how I could get back to the house in the woods without causing angry objections and recriminations. But nothing— no idea or plan—came, so I finally picked up my book and started reading. It was a long historical novel about the English king Harold of Hastings, the one who fell to William the Conqueror. It was wonderful and I got totally lost in it. Then I heard a door open and I came out of the spell. As I did so, I saw on my bureau two plates, two glasses and one napkin-wrapped knife.

I stared at them in dismay. I don't know how many dishes came with the cottage, but if there weren't many, those on the bureau would be missed before Ingrid had been downstairs long enough to set the table. Pulling on my jeans and a fresh T-shirt, I started downstairs barefoot, carrying the plates and the glasses, praying Ingrid had not had time to get downstairs. I should have known better.

"Ah ha!" she said with revolting cheeriness. "A midnight feast!" I waited for the next comment, which would be about my weight. "I used to have midnight feasts," she said. "What did you have?"

I put the two dishes down in the sink and wondered whether to admit that Morgan had been with me. Something made me decide not to. "Peanut butter and jelly," I said.

"Piggy!" Marian said, coming in from the porch, where she had obviously heard everything. "Bridget is a pi-ig!" sang Liza, who had been there, too.

"I thought you were going on a diet," Daddy said from the living room door.

Ingrid threw me a glance. "Shoo, everybody!" she said. "Unless you want to help! Yes, I think everybody can help. Marian, you set the table, Liza, you start pouring the cereal into the bowls. Bridget, put on the water to boil. I wonder where Morgan is."

I held my breath. At that moment Morgan appeared in the doorway.

"Bridget is a piggy biggy," Liza sang, setting out the cereal bowls.

I was so busy envisioning Liza being slowly lowered

41

into boiling oil that I wasn't watching Morgan and I missed what was happening until it happened. Morgan, head lowered, butted Liza in the stomach. Liza gave a shriek and clutched her middle. The cereal box flew out of her hand, knocking one of the bowls onto the floor, where it broke. Cereal scattered everywhere.

There was a dead silence.

"Morgan—" Daddy began.

Morgan ran out of the room and I heard the front door slam.

"Morgan!" Daddy's fist came down on the table.

"He was just sticking up for me," I said. "You can't punish him!"

"What do you mean, I can't?"

"Bridget," Ingrid said, "go and find Morgan. I don't think he should be running out on the road or into the woods by himself."

As I left I could hear Father going on about Morgan. I was pretty sure where Morgan would be heading and I took off after him.

As I expected, I found Morgan treading through the woods towards what I'd come to call the house in the woods.

"Morgan," I said, putting my hand on his shoulder and forcing him to stop, "first of all, thanks for sticking up for me." I bent down and kissed the top of his head, then made myself say, "I don't think Liza was trying to be nasty, but that doesn't mean I didn't want to kick her." I paused. "We're going to have to go back now."

As he shook his head and started forward I said, "Look, if we go there now, they're going to find out, one way or another. If we don't show up, then they'll call the police or the neighbors or somebody and one of them is sure to mention the house in the woods. And if Ingrid or Dad finds out about that, then they'll forbid our going and keep a watch on us." Gently I shook his shoulder. "Do you understand that?"

He pushed my hand away. For a moment I could tell it was a toss-up whether he'd let himself listen to me or go into one of his rages.

"I want to go there as much as you do," I said.

As we stood there while some kind of battle went on inside him, I heard the twitter of the birds up in the trees and the gentle sound of the wind making the leaves and branches move. We were only a few feet inside the woods, yet it was as though we were miles inside and the rest of the world far away.

Finally, under my hand, I felt his shoulder relax. He turned and we started back.

I realized then that I had to find a way for us to return to that house in the woods—for me as well as for Morgan. I knew because I had seen in the brief time we had been there that Morgan seemed happier and more at peace. And I had to go back because there was something urgently pulling me. No matter what obstacles were put in our way by Daddy or Ingrid, there was no way we could *not* return.

—6—

When Morgan and I got back, nothing much was said. Since Morgan couldn't talk, neither Ingrid nor Daddy could insist that he apologize to Liza, although on occasions like this in the past Daddy or whoever was looking after us would sometimes say, "Morgan, are you sorry you were rude?" and Morgan would usually nod.

I was half expecting something of that sort but hoped it wouldn't happen, because Morgan was in a touchier mood than he'd been in for some time and he seemed to dislike any suggestion Ingrid made. He and I sat down and ate our cereal in silence. Afterwards Liza came over and said rather grudgingly, "I didn't mean to be rude. I was just kidding." And she glared at Morgan.

I took a breath. "I know. It's just that being fat is the one thing people seem to think it's okay to make comments about."

Having done what she'd probably been told to do, Liza promptly made it worse. "But you can do something about being fat."

"Can you? Maybe someday you'll get fat, then we can all watch to see what you do about it."

I glanced at Daddy, waiting for him to say something,

44

since my weight was one of his favorite topics, too, but he surprised me. He said,

> "There's so much good in the worst of us,
> And so much bad in the best of us,
> That it hardly behooves any of us
> To talk about the rest of us."

"I didn't say she was bad," Liza protested. "I only said—" But she caught my eye at that moment. "Never mind," she muttered crossly.

"Where did you learn that?" I asked Daddy.

He lifted his head from his sailing book long enough to say, "Granny used to say that when I was a boy."

"Your grandmother?" Ingrid asked.

Daddy didn't answer right away. His attention was back on his book. Then, "No, my mother."

"But she wasn't really Bridget's—" Ingrid stopped.

I turned to her. "You keep saying things like that, making me feel like I don't belong."

Blood rushed up to her face. "I didn't mean—it's just that you're . . . well . . . adopted."

Daddy said nothing. His head was back in the book. If Mother were here, I thought, and somebody said that, she'd be on them right away, making them understand. And did Daddy do the same thing then? The thing was, it was always Mother. Daddy was distant. I had always assumed he felt the same way about not making a difference between me and the other children when they started to arrive. But I realized in that moment, standing there, that I couldn't actually remember him saying anything about my being as much a part of the family as Liza and Marian and Morgan. Except of course Morgan was different, too. The reason was not the same, but the effect was the same.

I was more determined than ever for Morgan and me to get back to the house in the woods as soon as possible.

Then, later that morning, Daddy's boat arrived, pulled on a trolley behind a car.

We all rushed out as Daddy and the man who brought it detached the trolley and rolled the boat down to the shore.

"Wow! What a terrific boat!" The words were shouted by a good-looking boy of about seventeen who was playing volleyball with Linda Martin and a couple of her brothers. "Linda, look!"

Linda turned and looked over the small line of rocks that divided our shore from theirs.

"Hey, that's neat!"

Suddenly a whole bunch of young people were pouring over to look at the boat.

"What kind is it?" one of them asked Daddy.

"It's a Sunfish."

"How many will it sail?"

Daddy sighed. "Not too many, I'm afraid. I'm not that experienced a sailor, so I thought I'd start small. Two adults, or one ordinary-sized adult and two small ones, or two children." He was leaning over the boat, running his hand over the mast which was lying along the top of the boat.

The man who brought it said, "Life jackets are under the deck here. Always make sure that any child who goes out wears one, and any adult too, I think. It's a good safeguard. I'll get the rollers out of the car."

"Rollers?" Daddy said. He had pulled up the mast so that it was now locked vertically into the small deck.

"Yeah, I told you, the canvas bags that you can put under the boat when you bring it ashore."

"Right, I remember."

"What's the number for?" the boy with Linda asked, pointing at the black digits printed on the sail.

"It's the registration number," the man said. He turned to Daddy. "Have you registered it up here yet?"

"No, I'll do that right away."

"Want me to take it out with you?" the man offered. He was big, dressed in jeans, with dark red hair and a kind face.

"Yes. I'd like that."

"Can I go, too?" Liza asked.

"And me?" Marian put in.

"Not this time," Daddy said, but he smiled at them, and I could see how pleased he was with their enthusiasm.

"I expect your father wants to get the feel of the boat first," Ingrid said.

"Well, when everybody else has had a try, I'd sure like to go out in it, sir," the good-looking boy said. He was very attractive, I thought, with fair wavy hair and hazel eyes.

"Absolutely," Daddy said.

He and the boatman got the Sunfish off the trolley and carried it down to the water, wading in to make sure there was enough depth. Except for Morgan and me, everybody followed them into the water, Ingrid in front. Luckily they all had on shorts, so they didn't get wet. Morgan was wearing shorts too, but I was in jeans. Shorts don't look too wonderful on someone of my shape, so I always wear slightly baggy jeans. I once learned from a woman in a store when I was trying on jeans and pants that anybody who is chubby is better off wearing something a little too large than too tight. "It's amazing," she said, sighing, "how hard it is to get that point across."

"I know," I said gloomily. "A small size in jeans is better for the ego than a loose larger size."

"That's what my daughter says."

I looked at the woman's thin build. "She doesn't take after you, I guess."

"No. She's like her father. But to listen to her, you'd assume it was an international plot."

I sympathized with her daughter's viewpoint. Ever since then I'd worn pants and jeans slightly on the roomy side. If something is a little loose, people sometimes think you've lost weight. But I never wore shorts.

So Morgan and I watched them run into the water. Suddenly I felt a tug on my arm. Morgan was pointing towards the woods.

I looked out over the water. This wasn't exactly the device I'd had in mind for getting back to the house. On the other hand, Daddy and the boatman, Ingrid, the twins, Linda and her boyfriend were all standing beside the boat, facing away from us.

"All right," I said. "Let's go. But we'd better be quick."

We ran. As we reached the other side of our cottage, I peered around the corner to see if anybody was watching our escape. But they were all still admiring the boat.

"We'll probably catch holy hell for this," I said to Morgan, as we sped across the road and up the bank.

But he streaked up ahead of me and then we were enclosed by the trees.

* * *

48

It was like coming home. When we got into the house we saw our friend there, again wearing her wide skirt, painting on a stand in front of her.

"Hello," she said.

Morgan ran up and stood beside her, looking at her painting. She turned and smiled at him. He put his hand on her arm, which is something he does when he wants to say he likes you, or even just say hello.

"Hi," she said to him.

I walked behind her. "Can I look today?"

"Yes. This is a painting I'm not particularly worried about, and it's almost done."

It was of a huge black cat just sitting on its haunches, its golden eyes staring ahead. There was something about the eyes in the cat face that made me sad, although I couldn't have said what it was. "Is it unhappy?"

"Yes. I'm glad you can see that. It's just lost its owner and is about to set out to find her."

"When you paint somebody who's sad, like the cat, do you know if somebody else can tell if it's sad?"

"No. That's why I was glad you could. Do you paint?"

"No. I can't draw."

"Are you sure?"

"Well, that's what the art teacher at school said, and at least two of my nannies."

She leaned forward suddenly and picked up a large flat book and opened it. "Here," she said, holding it out. "Draw something on that."

"But I told you, I can't."

She looked at me. "I didn't say draw something perfectly. I just said draw something."

"Like what?"

49

"Like that cat or those kittens, or whatever happens to be in your head at the moment." And she handed me a pencil.

I became irritated. I hated to be shown up for trying to do something I wasn't good at. "I'll do it in a minute." Then I went over to where Morgan was sitting by the big mother cat, gently stroking her between her ears. Her eyes were closed and a low rumble was coming from her. Her kittens were asleep in a box that was lined with what looked like someone's old sweater.

"What does she eat?" I asked.

"Well, she hunts," the woman said.

I suddenly realized I still didn't know what the woman's name was, but I decided I liked it better that way.

I looked up at her. "Do you bring them extra stuff?"

"Yes, but I'm not sure I'm doing them a favor. If I get busy or have to go away and can't come here regularly, what'll happen to them?"

I stared at the peaceful cat for a while, then I opened the drawing book and drew a line, representing the curve of her back as she lay there. Then I drew a few more lines—her ears and her tail. It looked awful. Angrily I tore the page off, crumpled it up and threw it away. It made a noise. The cat opened her eyes and jumped up. Then she spat. Morgan turned around and glared at me.

I decided to go upstairs. I was sure it would be better than it was the last time. But first, I decided, I'd look around the rest of the downstairs.

First I went into a room that looked like it might have been a dining room. There was a sort of broken-down sideboard, but no table and only two chairs.

The paper was peeling from the walls there, too, and there were more light patches where pictures had once hung. Then I went through to the kitchen. All the fittings around the sink were either broken or rusty. I opened one of the cupboard doors and saw a stream of ants walking in rows along one of the shelves. Suddenly I heard a scuttling noise and little feet scrabbled along the floor. There was a wild flurry and the cat sailed past my legs and pounced on something. I saw then that the poor struggling creature was a mouse.

"No!" I screamed. As I tried to get the cat's mouth off the mouse I felt claws rake my arm.

Suddenly a hand pulled me back and turned me around. "That's her lunch," the woman said. "You can't deny it to her."

"But it's cruel and horrible!"

"How would you like somebody to remove a piece of chicken or a steak from your plate just as you were about to eat it? After all, somebody had to kill those creatures so you could have your dinner."

I shook her hand off my arm and stood fighting tears. The mouse had somehow gotten away for a moment, but the cat pounced again. "No," I said.

But she took my arm. "Come, come along back here. You're bleeding."

I looked down at my other arm and saw three lines of blood. My head was in a muddle. I knew the woman was right, but all I could think about was the poor mouse. "I feel so rotten for the mouse. It must have been terrified!"

"Yes. But maybe some kind of numbness takes over. I've been told that. I don't know whether it's true or not."

I saw Morgan staring first at my arm and then towards

51

the cat's tail, which was all that was visible on the other side of the old refrigerator.

The woman moved so she could see all of the cat. "Well, you'll be glad to hear that the mouse evidently got away down its hole."

I went over and looked. The cat was staring at a hole in the old boarding; her tail was switching.

"I'm going to get some paper and stuff it in the hole," I said.

"You do know, don't you, that if the mother cat isn't fed, she won't be able to feed her kittens. She's doing what she is supposed to do: think of her family first."

"That's not what my mother—my real mother— did," I said, anger pouring out of me like a stream of hot coals.

"How so? Come along back to the living room. You'll feel better there."

I didn't want to do what she or anyone else suggested, but I went.

"What did you mean when you said that?" the woman asked, putting aside her stick and sitting back down in her chair.

I really didn't want to answer, but I didn't seem to have any choice. "She gave me up for adoption," I said.

"I see." She picked up her paintbrush, put it in a small container of water on an upturned box near her stand, then wiped it off. "Perhaps it was the best thing for her to do for you."

"Why?"

"I don't know, but I could make a few guesses. She might not have been able to afford to bring you up, especially if she had to work; she might have felt unable to give you the things she thought you should have."

"Yeah. That's what everyone says."

"So you've discussed this before?"

I didn't answer right away. Then I said, "Mother—my adoptive mother—said it. I haven't talked to anybody else about it. But I've read some books."

"Do you remember your birth mother at all?"

I shook my head. "No, I was only two when I was adopted so I don't remember anything before that."

"Have you talked recently to your adoptive mother about it?"

"No. She died when I was nine and Morgan was two."

"I see."

I expected her to go on with her questions, but she didn't, so I said grudgingly, "We—Morgan, the twins and I—have had nannies since."

"And your father? Have you talked to him about it?"

"I think he's sorry he adopted me."

It was incredible, I thought. I was saying to this strange woman things I had often thought but hadn't said to anybody. I looked over and saw Morgan was staring at me. If she was like most grown-ups, I thought, she'd now say she was sure I was wrong. But she didn't. What she finally said was, "Morgan loves you."

I saw him smile suddenly.

"Yes," I said. "He does. How did you know?" But I realized it was a silly question before I asked. I knew she knew.

At that moment the cat walked back into the room, went over to the box of kittens, pulled out one and started licking it. She licked it all over. The others tumbled out then and started mewing. She lay down and stretched out and they all fought for a place and a nipple each. I thought about the mouse she didn't catch. Maybe she was hungry. I'd bring her stuff, too, I thought.

I picked up the book again and started to draw another line that was to be the cat's back.

"Just do it for yourself, not because you're going to show it to anyone or let anyone tell you whether they like it or not."

But I didn't like the line. So I put the book down and decided to try going upstairs again.

"Be careful," the woman said. "The stairs are creaky."

I got up safely and started down the hall. It was like walking against a wall of water that was trying to push me back. A terrible feeling came over me and I wanted to cry. "This is stupid," I said aloud. "I can go where I like." I was determined to explore the upstairs rooms no matter what. I pushed my way into the first room. There was almost nothing in it—just a bureau, a table and a chair. I forced myself to walk around the room and then out. I felt sick and had a headache, but I went into the next one. It had a bed with covers on it. There was a bureau here, too, and a set of bookshelves. It was easier to walk in here. I went over to the bookshelf and pulled a book out. A huge cloud of dust rose and swirled. My hands were covered with it. I looked at the title, which was almost invisible. *The Wind in the Willows*. I'd heard of it, of course, but I'd never read it.

I opened the book cover. At the top of the page in straight up-and-down handwriting was the name Catherine Bingham.

"Catherine Bingham," I said aloud. Who was Catherine Bingham?

The bed suddenly looked inviting. I went over, pushed the pillows up, sat on the bed and started reading.

— 7 —

I was walking down a long hall, following something—a tall something in white. I started to run and then the something turned around and picked me up and a great wave of happiness went over me. That happiness seemed for a while to envelop me in a warm blue sea. After that, and with no warning, there was a change. I was not being held. I was hiding behind something or in something in a state of terror. There was a terrible noise and I was convinced I would die and be dead forever. So I tried to cry out, but my voice didn't work, and I couldn't get out of wherever I was and there was no one in the world to hear me. All I could do was cry. . . .

"That must have been a bad dream," the woman said. She was standing beside the bed, her hand on my arm. For a moment I didn't know who she was or where I was.

"What happened?" I said.

"You started to cry out. So we came up to see what was going on."

I saw Morgan then, behind her. His face was pinched and unhappy. "It's all right, Morgan," I said. "It was a dream."

"What was the dream?" the woman asked.

It was still vivid in my head. "I was following a tall

woman in white. She picked me up and made me feel wonderful, but I couldn't see her face. Then I was in a small room or maybe a closet, and there was a horrible, horrible noise outside, so I screamed, only I thought nobody heard me and I'd never get out. Then I woke up. Or you woke me up."

"Have you ever had that dream before?"

Funny, I thought. Now that she'd put it into words, I knew I had. "Yes. But I'd forgotten it."

"Do you have any idea what it means? What it's about?"

I shook my head, "No."

After a minute she got up. "Well, I'm going back to my painting." She picked up her stick from the floor and went out, her long skirt almost touching the floor. After a minute, Morgan followed her.

I went on lying there, filled with sadness. After a while I realized I was crying. Then I felt myself getting drowsy, and forced myself to sit up. I didn't want to go to sleep again.

When I got downstairs, Morgan, the cat beside him, was sitting on the floor painting from a small dish on which there were dabs of several colors. He wasn't drawing anything, he was just pulling a big paintbrush dipped in various colors across a large piece of paper. He looked absorbed and happy.

I went over to the woman. I thought about asking her her name, but couldn't make myself say the words. It was as though I felt safety or happiness or something was in not knowing. But I said, "Can I have a piece of paper, too? And maybe a pencil?"

Without saying anything she took a pencil from a collection lying on the overturned box and ripped off a couple of sheets from her drawing pad. She handed them all over with a smile. "You might need this," she added, and gave me a block of thick cardboard to put under the paper.

I sat in the big chair, which gave off a huge puff of dust, and started to draw the cat again. I made myself remember what the woman had said: "Do it for yourself, not because you're going to show it to anyone." The drawing seemed to go better, or maybe I didn't want so much for it to be perfect.

I don't know how long we'd been there when I became aware suddenly that the sun, which had been faintly visible through one filthy window, was now trying to come through another, equally dirty window. Obviously it had changed places. I jumped up. "We have to go, Morgan, or they'll start looking."

When I went over I saw he was surrounded by several pieces of paper from the woman's pad, all covered with colors. I stared at them. There was no design and no shape, just wild blobs and streaks in different colors or combined colors. But I was surprised to see some made me feel happy and some angry.

"That's nice," I said, not knowing quite why I said it. I'd never liked the pieces of nonobjective art that we were shown at school. They didn't mean anything. But I did like these. Maybe it was because they were Morgan's.

"We have to go," I said again, and bent down to pick up some of the paintings.

The next thing I knew Morgan was flying at me. He pushed me violently and I staggered back and fell.

"What—" I got up. "What did you do that for? I could have hurt myself!"

He was staring at me, the paintings in his hand. Then he went over to the woman and gave them to her.

"What do you want me to do with them, Morgan?" she asked.

He bent down and put them back into the pad and then handed the pad to her.

"Keep them?" she said.

He nodded.

"All right, but if I do that, I think you ought to show you're sorry to your sister." She turned to me. "I take it you are his sister."

"In a way," I said bitterly. "I'm adopted. He isn't. He belongs . . ."

"And you don't?"

"I don't feel like I do." I paused. "I've never actually said that before."

She smiled. "I wonder if it's me or the house or just being away from—well, away from whatever you're used to." Then she added quickly, "But maybe it's none of those things."

Morgan came over, put his hand on my arm, then hugged me.

"Did you think I was going to do something to your paintings?"

He nodded. "Destroy them?" I asked surprised.

He shook his head.

"Maybe take them with us?"

He nodded.

I sighed. "I wouldn't do that, I don't think."

I bent down and picked up my own efforts. Tiger looked a little more like Tiger.

"Why don't you bring them here and put them back in the pad along with Morgan's?"

For a minute I thought I'd just tear them up, but I finally took them to her pad and pushed them in under Morgan's. "Come on, Morgan," I said.

I'd forgotten to put on my watch, so I had no idea what time it was. We walked back to the cottage and

59

found Ingrid in the kitchen, making sandwiches and cooking some soup.

"You missed a wonderful morning," she said reprovingly. "We all had a sail. Your father took the twins out after he got back with the boatman, then I went, then Linda's boyfriend. Where were you?"

I'd prepared an answer. "We took a long walk along the shore and the woods further along," and I pointed in the direction away from the house in the woods, towards the shore and the section where the trees rimmed the rocks and the water.

"I do think you ought to stay with the rest of us more. It would please your father if you showed some interest in his boat. After all, he got it for the family."

"He didn't ask us if we wanted a boat," I said. I could hear the angry note in my voice.

"You don't know what some young people would do to be able to sail." Ingrid said. "A boat is a luxury most people can't afford. You're very lucky."

"I get seasick," I said, making it up on the spur of the moment.

She looked at me. "I didn't know you'd ever been out on a boat."

"Oh yes," I said vaguely, and then added, "at camp one summer."

"Well, that's no real problem. I have Dramamine and can give you some."

"I don't think people should take drugs," I said virtuously, and knew I should have kept my mouth shut.

"It's not a drug, not in the way most people use the word," she said. "Why are you always so difficult?"

"Do you want help with the sandwiches?" I asked.

After a moment she said, "Yes. You can slice some of that turkey breast and the cheese over there."

It occurred to me to ask why she got cheese that had to be sliced when you could buy cheese already sliced

60

with paper in between the slices. But I'd argued enough. I didn't want her making any more difficulty about Morgan and me going out.

After a while Daddy, the twins and Linda's boyfriend came in, crossing the veranda into the kitchen.

"That's a little gem of a boat," Daddy said. "Even I can manage her! Bridget, you and Morgan missed a great opportunity. But you can go out with me this afternoon."

It had been easy for me to tell Ingrid I didn't like sailing. It wouldn't be so easy to say the same thing to Daddy. I glanced at Ingrid, who was looking at me.

Then she said, "I want some of us to go into the village this afternoon. There's a lot of stuff we need and I could use some extra hands to help."

I didn't trust Ingrid, but I knew she was making it easy for me. "Morgan and I'll go, Ingrid. There are a couple of things I have to get."

"Can we go out again, Daddy?" the twins said in chorus, jumping up and down.

"I have to go to town, too," Linda's boyfriend said. "But I'd love to go out later if you run out of passengers, sir."

Daddy smiled at him and then at the twins. "With the twins and their enthusiasm, I don't think we're going to do that. But you're very welcome, anyway." He glanced at me. "Certainly landlubbers are not going to be forced to do something most people would turn cartwheels to do."

"What's his name?" I asked when Linda's boyfriend left.

"He's cute, isn't he?" Marian said, and fluttered her eyelashes at me.

"Not especially," I replied.

"Steve McKay," Daddy said. "He seems like a good

kid. He said he hadn't sailed before, but he sure picked it up fast.''

The village turned out to be partly a pretty New England town with a main street, a green, a white frame town hall, a library and colonial-looking houses in streets leading off the main street. But just beyond the old town were a couple of motels and a mall containing a huge supermarket, a hamburger joint, a fried chicken place, an ice cream parlor, a bookstore, a video store. We drove through the main part of the town and parked in the mall.

Morgan and I went with Ingrid into the supermarket. She gave me a list, so he and I set off with one cart and she went with another and her own list.

When we got the things stowed into the car I said to Ingrid, ''Are you going to any other store?''

She shook her head. ''No, this is all I came in for.''

''Well, I'd like to stay and look at the town. Are you going to come back?''

''No, I hadn't planned to. You should have told me first, and I could have waited a while. As it is, there's frozen stuff in the groceries and I can't just leave it in the trunk of the car.''

I started to make some grumbling comment when I remembered that she had helped me out at lunch. ''Maybe we can walk,'' I said.

''It's five miles.'' Then she added, ''Oh, all right. I'll come back for you in a couple of hours. Will you find enough to entertain yourselves that long?''

''Yes. Thanks, Ingrid.''

Then she knocked my gratitude flying by saying in her carrying, rather emphatic voice, ''I really don't think you ought to go and eat something like ice cream. Your lunch was healthy and well balanced and not too high in calories. You must learn to watch your diet.''

A bunch of young people just happened to be passing the car at that moment. Some of them turned and looked at me. One of the boys nudged the girl next to him and said something. The girl looked at me and giggled.

"Thanks," I said furiously. "Couldn't you have said it louder? The whole parking lot could have had a good laugh."

She opened her mouth, then closed it, got in the car, slamming the door, and drove off.

Maybe because she said what she did, or maybe I would have anyway, we went and had ice cream cones. I was half expecting the same bunch of teenagers to pass by and was ready with a smart-aleck comment, but they didn't.

Then Morgan pointed to the video game store, so we went there and I let him play while I checked out some of the videos and thought about suggesting to Daddy that we get a VCR. Then we went into the bookstore which turned out to be a good one, filled with paperbacks of all kinds and for all ages, and I browsed happily there, spending more money than I should have. But books were the path through the looking glass, to the other world I was always looking for, the world where I was somebody else. Then, although I knew I shouldn't, I let Morgan go back to the video store while I went to the town library, which was in the main part of the old town. The librarian was nice and let me look around. I saw stacks of the local paper and many more books. So I got a temporary library card and took out more books. It was when I was walking back towards the mall to pick up Morgan that I saw Linda. She was in a car parked off the main street in a kind of alleyway. Only shops looked down on the car and it was under a tree. Why I noticed her I don't know, but I looked in the back window as I passed, and I recognized her immediately. It wasn't hard. She was one of the prettiest girls I'd met, with a lot of blonde curly hair. She knew she was attractive, and I wasn't about to forget the way she ignored me.

Anyway, she was in the back of the car, necking furiously. Only the boy with her wasn't Steve. He was another, tough-looking kid, who turned around and stared at me as I stared at them.

Then I walked on with a mixed feeling of satisfaction and anger: satisfaction because I had caught her out, anger because she had pretended I wasn't there. I wondered what Ingrid would say if I told her. But I knew I wouldn't.

Then I ran to pick up Morgan.

—8—

The days fell into a pattern. Morgan and I would manage to go to the house in the woods at least once during the day. When we didn't go to the house, we played volleyball or some other game on the beach with Linda, Steve and some of the other kids or went into town or made sand castles, something Morgan seemed to like increasingly. His castles got more and more elaborate, and he started modeling smaller figures that looked vaguely like animals. We met some of the kids from cottages further down the beach on the other side, and discovered that a pier jutting from one of the houses and partly hidden from our house by trees was a sort of hanging-out place for the kids who weren't occupied doing something else. There were rowboats there, a raft anchored out in the lake where people who swam could sunbathe and a little hut at the land end of the pier.

After we learned about the pier, when Ingrid or Daddy wanted to know what Morgan and I were doing when they were planning to go out on the boat, it was easy to say casually, "Going down to the pier." I was afraid at first that they wouldn't be enthusiastic, or insist on taking us to see what was going on. But Daddy had become absolutely fixated on the boat. And he had a whole bunch of people who wanted to go out all the time—

65

Ingrid, Steve, the twins, Linda (sometimes) and some of the other kids.

The first time I saw Linda after the car incident I waited to see how she would act. As near as possible she pretended I wasn't there or, when she thought I was watching her, would suddenly start talking to someone or laughing with them. But I knew she was aware of me, and was aware of what I had seen. Often I wondered who the boy was. It was hard to say, after that one brief look, why he looked different from the other boys around the lake. But he did. And without either of us mentioning it, I knew Linda didn't want me to tell anyone about it. It became a sort of game the two of us played without either of us mentioning it. When she was at home or at the pier or playing games on our beach, she was nearly always with Steve, who seemed to like her a lot. I found myself feeling sorry on his behalf, but then I told myself to shut up. Boys as attractive as Steve weren't attracted by overweight girls of fourteen. And if I were in any doubt about it, I had plenty of barbs from Daddy and Ingrid to help me remember.

"Bridget, I really think you ought to get more vigorous exercise. It would help with your weight. And you want to lose it now, you know. You're getting towards adulthood and it's a proven fact that if you can't get rid of puppy fat while you're young you'll be struggling with it for the rest of your life."

"Yes, Daddy," I said, raging inside. The house in the woods had become so important that I was willing to give up all my other battles to keep his or Ingrid's attention off where Morgan and I went.

"We might see if there are some exercise classes in town," Ingrid said, putting some butter on the table as we were sitting down to breakfast. "By the way, that's not butter, it's whipped margarine—less saturated fat and fewer calories."

"She'll make you lose somehow!" Marian crowed happily. She was as tan as her sandals.

"I bet you have to diet anyway!" Liza said, helping herself to the de-caloried fake butter.

I saw Morgan's hand go out to his glass, and something made me catch his wrist. I stared into his angry eyes, then put his hand down onto the table. How I knew he was going to hurl his milk at Liza I didn't know. But I was pretty sure that's exactly what he had been going to do. I held his hand for a moment, feeling the tears behind my eyes. Morgan might be only seven, mute and given to uncontrollable rages, but he knew me better than anyone else, and at least some of those rages were on my behalf.

Evidently Daddy came out of his sailing trance long enough to say in a much kinder voice, "How about you and me going sailing this morning, Bridget? You'll see how much fun it is. I know if you're afraid of being seasick Ingrid will give you some medicine to forestall it."

I looked down at my lap, again moved in a way that surprised me. If only—if only I didn't have a wild fear of being somewhere I couldn't leave if I had to. I got panicked at the thought of being in a small boat in the middle of a lake, and of having to stay there, no matter what. I could swim, but not well enough to jump overboard if the feeling of being trapped which I hated so much came over me. I told Ingrid I had sailed at camp, and I had, once. I was literally sick with fright until the boat got back to shore. Claustrophobia, the camp counselor called it. She said she'd write to my parents. Mother was dead at the time, of course. Whether Daddy ever got the letter I don't know. He never mentioned it, and I never went to camp again. The only person I told about it was Morgan.

"Well?" Daddy said now. I looked up. The kind,

friendly look he'd had was gone. He was now getting angry. What excuse could I give? What would he accept? That I'd promised to take Morgan into town? That I didn't feel well? Since I'd just eaten lunch I wasn't too sure how well he'd take that.

Then Morgan saved me. He gave a shout and pushed the milk pitcher off the table.

"Of all the stupid things—" Daddy said angrily, starting out of his chair.

Ingrid jumped to her feet. "Morgan! That is inexcusably careless! Now you'll just have to get a cloth from the kitchen! Oh, never mind—I'll do it!" And she ran into the kitchen.

"Butterfingers!" Liza said.

Gratefully, I bent down and started to try and soak up some of the milk with the paper napkins from the table. "It's all right, Morgan," I said quietly.

"No, it's not all right," Daddy almost shouted. "I really think it's time we considered—"

The horrible specter of an institution for Morgan seemed to fill my mind. "No," I said, and was at the point of saying Morgan had done it deliberately to save me when Ingrid flew back, a sponge in one hand and a bucket and cloth in the other.

"It won't be so bad if we can just get it up now. Morgan, I'm sorry. I know it was an accident. I didn't mean to speak sharply!" Ingrid said.

Morgan was standing right behind me, his hand on my arm.

For a moment I wondered if it would be better for Morgan if I said Yes, he did mean to do it, or No, he didn't.

But at that point Daddy flung down his napkin and stalked out onto the porch and then down onto the beach towards the boat.

"Why don't you go with him?" Ingrid said.

68

I thought about going and trying to explain to Daddy about Morgan and how I felt about being in a boat. But I knew I couldn't.

By this time the twins were out with Daddy and the boat. Ingrid looked out at them for a moment, then said, "I think I'll leave the dishes for the moment. I'm pretty sure there'll be room for me as well."

When they'd gone I looked at Morgan. "Thanks," I said, and bent down and kissed him on the head. "You know, maybe it'd be a good thing if we at least put the dishes in the dishwasher before we go to the house. What do you think?"

He nodded.

We cleared the table, gave a final swipe to the soggy rag carpet, rinsed off the dishes and put them into the dishwasher. Then I put some detergent into the little container in the dishwasher and started it going. "Okay, let's go now!" I said.

The woman wasn't there when we got to the house, and I felt terribly disappointed. I think Morgan did, too. We stood in the big dark room for a minute.

"Maybe she'll come later," I said.

I knew I was using her batteries when I went over and turned on her light. "I'll ask her what batteries she's using and bring some next time," I said, salving my conscience. Her paint box was there, closed. Her little pot of water was covered and her paintbrushes neatly laid out on the upturned box, along with some pencils. Her big sketch pad was on the floor to one side, with Morgan's and my paintings and drawings sticking out.

"I don't think we ought to open her box and use her paints," I said. "How would you like to draw instead? Using her pencils would be all right."

He scowled.

"Morgan, she's been really nice to us. I'll get you some paints or crayons in the village, so we'll have them. Come on, let me give you a pencil."

He didn't look too happy, but I settled him in the chair with the cardboard and two sheets of paper from the woman's book. Then I decided to explore the rest of the house some more. But I'd avoid the room where I had had that awful dream.

I moved carefully, first around the downstairs and then upstairs. Cobwebs hung in the corners of the ceiling and I heard small scuttling feet. Sometimes they belonged to the kittens who were beginning to run around. Sometimes they didn't, and I thought about the mouse that the cat caught and my horror at the scene. But the woman was right. The cat's first job was to feed her family, and if it meant the death of the poor mouse, I had to remember that. After all, as the woman had reminded me, cattle died when I ate steak or wore leather shoes. It didn't make me happy to think about that, but to start being a vegetarian now, at the summer cottage, with everything else going wrong, would tip Daddy over from periodic irritation with me to—

To what?

I didn't know. I walked slowly from room to room, trying to picture the people who must once have lived here. It wasn't hard. It was almost as though they were still there, around me, just on the other side of . . . of the looking glass. And as I walked, I knew what, in that other world—the world I lived in most of the time with Daddy and Ingrid and the twins—I was most afraid of: One day Daddy would be so angry with me he'd tell me I wasn't his daughter, that he'd never wanted to adopt me, and that he was sorry he had.

I was upstairs in a sort of study when I imagined that scene. It was so real, I could see his face, hear his voice. I sat down on a hard chair in front of what looked like a desk. A terrible feeling of despair came over me. The desk, which had a flap top, was closed. Without thinking I lowered the flap and leaned my elbows on it. I found myself staring at cubbyholes filled with old envelopes and pieces of paper. A huge spider ran out from one of the cubbyholes. I cried out and sprang up. Then I ran out of the room. As I did so a board in the hall seemed to move under my feet.

I'll die here, I thought. But the strange part was, although I felt frightened it was entirely different from the fear I felt at the thought of sailing. That was just plain fear. What was this? I didn't know, but it was something else—more like entering a room that I already knew, that I had been in before, that I desperately feared going into again.

* * *

When Morgan and I got back, the others hadn't returned yet from their sail. Then I looked again, and saw the boat up on the rollers. "I wonder where they all are?" I said aloud.

Morgan came up and pointed back towards the house in the woods. "Yes, Morgan, I'd like to go back, too, but let's not push our luck."

A minute later I heard the door on the front porch open and Daddy, Ingrid, the twins, Linda, Steve and another couple Daddy's age all came into the house from the road side.

"You missed a marvelous sail!" Liza chirped.

"In a humongous great boat," Marian said.

"This is Dr. and Mrs. Brinton," Daddy said, "and these"—he indicated Morgan and me—"are Morgan and Bridget."

"Hi!" I said, feeling rather shy.

"Hi," Mrs. Brinton said. She looked at Morgan. "Have you had a nice morning?"

Morgan nodded. He looked wary.

"We went for a walk along the shore," I said.

"That's funny," Dr. Brinton commented. "We sailed along the shore near here and didn't see you."

"We were in the woods," I said quickly.

He smiled. "You should have come with us. It was a perfect day for sailing, wasn't it, kids?"

"Yes!" the chorus of the twins, Linda and Steve said loudly.

"Bridget doesn't like to sail," Liza said.

"Oh?" Mrs. Brinton said. "Why not?" She paused a minute. "Are you afraid of the water?"

"No," I said loudly.

"She gets seasick, I'm afraid," Ingrid said.

Mrs. Brinton smiled. "Oh, you can take some medicine for that. We have plenty, for people who have that trouble. You can come and get it when you need to. We're just around the curve of the lake. You can't see our house from here; it's hidden by that sort of peninsula with trees. But it's not far."

"I've offered her Dramamine," Daddy said flatly. "She doesn't want it."

His sentence lay there. I felt Morgan's hand creep into mine. "And how about you?" Dr. Brinton said, looking at Morgan. "Wouldn't you like to come out with us next time?"

Morgan shook his head. There was a short silence. "Morgan doesn't talk," I said.

"I see."

There was another silence. They were laughing and having a good time when they came in, I thought. But Morgan and I seemed to stop that. Suddenly I hated them, and myself—and Morgan? I glanced down at him. No, never Morgan.

"Can we help you with lunch?" I asked Ingrid.

"Yes, as a matter of fact, you can. I'm going to fix a

large salad and we'll have cold cuts. Why don't you start putting the greens in the salad bowl.''

Later, when we were sitting down, I said to Dr. Brinton, ''You must have a big boat.''

He laughed. ''Yes. It's my great weakness. I've gone from a Sunfish to one that can carry this whole crowd. Maybe some day you'll feel like coming out.''

''Maybe,'' I said, cursing myself for bringing up the subject of the boat.

After that the conversation went to other subjects. I sat and listened. It's true, I thought, I don't belong in this family, and I started having a fantasy about how Morgan and I would, one day, just leave and live by ourselves. When I tried to think of a place we'd go, the obvious one loomed huge in my mind: the house in the woods. I let myself think about that for a while, pushing back awkward questions such as what would we eat, where would we go to school.

''Bridget!''

I jumped. ''Sorry,'' I muttered.

''With a concentration like that, you could be a great poet or a great scientist!'' Dr. Brinton said.

''Did you say something to me?'' I asked. ''I'm sorry, I didn't hear.''

''That's because you weren't listening,'' Daddy said, and then seemed to bite his lip. He forced a smile. ''You do go off into fantasy land sometimes, don't you?''

''Sometimes I wish I could,'' Ingrid said.

Linda, Steve and the twins seemed to be having a conversation of their own.

''Well, that's the other thing to do,'' Steve was saying. ''There are some good horse farms around here.''

''I haven't seen any horses,'' I said. I loved all animals, but I particularly loved horses, although I had never ridden. We'd never been anyplace where I could. But most of my calendars have been horse calendars.

"They're further down the road on the other side."

"Do you ride?" I asked Dr. Brinton.

"No, my wife and son are the riders. I sail. Do you like to ride?"

"I've never ridden," I said.

"If she's spooked by going out on a boat, I don't see why she'd like riding a horse," Liza said. "They're much more dangerous!"

"Who told you that?" Mrs. Brinton asked, sounding amused.

"Well," Liza said. I knew she hadn't thought of an answer. But I also knew that wouldn't stop her. "I thought everyone knew that."

"I don't think it's necessarily true. Whether more people get thrown from a horse than knocked off a boat depends, I guess, on how many people sail versus ride. Dangerwise, there's probably not a lot to choose between them.

"Of course, there's Elissa Hamilton, who taught at the horse farm that I use. She got tossed at the beginning of the summer and still has to use a cane."

I looked up quickly and saw Morgan's face across the table, interested and intensely curious. He fixed his eyes on me, and I knew he wanted me to ask the question.

"What happened to her?" I asked casually.

"She was teaching a newcomer, who didn't really know how to manage her horse. Anyway, the newcomer's horse reared in front of Elissa's, and her horse then reared and took off."

"I guess that took care of her riding for the summer," Daddy said.

"No, surprisingly not. I don't think she goes out as much as she did, and she can't teach or school horses as much as she did, but the injury was to her foot rather than her leg. She can still get herself up on the horse, though she has to use a mount. But I think she can't stay

74

up all day. Which, considering she's part owner of the farm, must put a crimp in her financial plans for the summer.''

"Is that what she does—is that her regular job, I guess I'm asking?'' Daddy said.

"Yes,'' Mrs. Brinton said. "Which is funny, considering how long she went to art school and presumably wanted to be an artist.''

"Why did she switch?'' I asked.

Mrs. Brinton didn't answer.

"Wasn't there some kind of a scandal?'' Dr. Brinton said. "Didn't she—''

"Will somebody pass me some more bread,'' Mrs. Brinton said firmly. "I find I'm starved.'' It was as though she were ringing down a curtain on the subject.

Liza's eyes were round with excitement. "But—''

"I've told you not to talk with your mouth full,'' Ingrid said.

— 9 —

For two days Morgan and I weren't able to go to the house in the woods. The next day we had a family picnic, which took practically all day because we drove around the lake to the other side and climbed, partly by car and partly on foot, halfway up one of the neighboring mountains. Then, on the way back, we visited a fairground near another lake and had dinner in town. The second day there was a sort of barbecue on the beach in front of the Martins' cottage.

I could feel Morgan's restlessness getting edgier and edgier. Any moment we were alone he tugged on my hand in a way that had come to mean, When can we go to the house in the woods?

"Not now," I'd whisper quickly. "If we tried to go now there'd be such a fuss we might never get there again." So, with that threat, he'd quiet down for a while. Luckily, he liked the fairground, particularly the scary rides on the roller coasters. But he didn't much like being with the other kids his age, who, when no adult was listening, would tease him.

"Hey, Morgan, come on, say something!" one kid named Ted, a little bigger than Morgan, said softly, dancing around him. "I bet you could if you tried. Or is your name really Moron?" And he giggled.

I saw Morgan's fist flash out and connect with Ted's

nose. Ted was about to ram him back when I went over and took him by the hair. "My, what a big brave boy you are, aren't you? I'll bet you pull wings off flies!"

"Let me go, fatstuff!" Ted screamed.

Steve came running over. "What the hell's going on?"

"She's pulling my hair," he yelled.

Steve looked at me.

I let go of Ted's hair, wondering if Steve had heard what Ted had called me. "Ted was bullying Morgan about not talking."

Ted rubbed his head. "What's it to you, fatstuff?"

"Only bullies and cowards tease people about their physical disabilities or appearances," Steve said. "And your parents will be sorry to hear that you're already getting known as a bully."

Ted stuck out his tongue, then ran off.

"Sorry about that," Steve said to me.

I felt completely humiliated. "Think nothing of it," I said as casually as I could. "It happens all the time. Come on, Morgan, let's go back on the carousel."

As we walked away I realized I hadn't thanked Steve. Who knows what might have happened to Morgan if he hadn't intervened? But all I could think about was that he had heard me called "fatstuff."

The next day at the barbecue I began to realize that Daddy was talking over Morgan's problem with Dr. Brinton. He and the doctor got off by themselves and when they glanced at Morgan for the third time, it was pretty clear.

"Is Daddy talking to Dr. Brinton about Morgan?" I asked Ingrid, when Morgan had gone off to play tag with some other kids his own age.

"You know your father wants the best for all of you," Ingrid said. "And he isn't happy with the treatment suggested for Morgan by the various doctors and psychiatrists he had consulted before.''

"He doesn't approve of psychiatry, anyway."

Ingrid didn't answer immediately, then said, "That's not entirely true. I think he feels that an awful lot of blaming the parents for everything has become fashionable and children are not expected to make any effort for themselves."

"Is Dr. Brinton a psychiatrist?"

Again Ingrid didn't answer at first. "He's some kind of therapist, I think. He's a sort of consultant at a . . . a children's hospital near here."

"A hospital or a psychiatric institution?" I asked sharply.

"Don't jump at me like that!" she said. "I think it's an institution."

I didn't say anything for a moment. I was feeling a little sick, the way I always felt when something about Morgan's being treated somewhere else came up. The same way I felt sick when I was confronted with something that made me realize how much my being adopted made a difference to Daddy or somebody like Ingrid.

Ingrid made a slight exasperated sound. "Now, don't get yourself into an uproar, Bridget. You know as well as I do, your father can't just let Morgan go on like this. He has to turn to anybody who has any ideas at all—any new ideas—as to what could be done."

At that point somebody came over and started talking about the food and didn't we want some salad, and Ingrid went off with her.

I was so upset I went and sat by myself at the open fire that had been built on the beach inside a sort of circle of stones. After a while I started imagining myself in the house in the woods, walking around.

I'd look in all the rooms, I'd let down the flap of the desk. I wouldn't go back into the room where I'd had the bad dream, but the other rooms were all right. Or maybe I would go back into the room and have another dream—only a good one this time, maybe a dream about whoever had lived there before and how they'd come back and I could make friends with them . . .

"Bridget!" somebody yelled. I jumped and looked up. It was Steve, holding a plate down towards me.

"Thanks," I said and took the plate.

Steve, who was holding a plate of his own, sat down beside me. "Man, you really phase out, don't you! Do you do that all by yourself—I mean, not taking anything?"

"No, of course I don't take anything," I said defensively. Somehow the fact that he was so good-looking made me feel worse. Like he was just being polite. A boy as attractive as Steve would never give me the time of day, I thought, only somebody like Linda. The moment I thought of her I remembered the other boy I'd seen her with. At that moment, as though a bell had gone off in my mind, I looked up and stared straight at Linda. She was watching me, her face taut.

I tried not to think how fat I felt and said to Steve, "I meant to thank you for . . . for helping out with Ted yesterday."

"It's okay. He's not a very nice kid. I wish he hadn't come here this summer. Morgan's not the only one he tries to push around."

I picked up the plastic fork and moved the food around a bit on the plate. "Where do you live the rest of the year?"

"In Westchester. Where do you live?"

"In Connecticut. Where does Linda live?" I asked.

"Connecticut somewhere. She tells me you're adopted. Is that true?"

I hadn't told her, but I supposed Ingrid or Daddy had contributed that to the local news grapevine. "Yes," I said. "So you see I don't really belong." I got up. "I'm not really hungry." I threw the paper plate with the food left on it into one of the big wire baskets lined with a plastic bag. Then I walked off, thinking how miserable I could make Steve if I told him what I knew about Linda.

The next morning Daddy said he and Ingrid were going sailing. He turned then to Morgan. "Wouldn't you like to come with us, Morgan?"

Morgan shook his head.

"How do you know you wouldn't like it?" Daddy asked. "You've never tried it, have you?"

Morgan didn't lift his eyes from his cereal nor did he nod or shake his head. He acted as though he hadn't heard.

"Have you?" Daddy suddenly said sharply.

Morgan, still not looking up, shook his head.

"I realize you don't talk," Daddy said. "But there's nothing wrong with your hearing, according to the many doctors who have tested you. So the least you can do is acknowledge a question."

Morgan kept his eyes down.

"Daddy," I said. "It's not something Morgan is doing deliberately. He—he can't help it."

"Then explain to me, Madame Therapist, if there's nothing wrong with him physically why he can't help not talking."

The trouble is, I couldn't. It was just something I could feel.

"There are more things in heaven and earth, Horatio," Ingrid said, getting up from the table and starting to pick up dishes.

I knew it was a quote, although I didn't know from where. Mainly I was grateful, and I smiled at her.

"Than are dreamt of in your philosophy," Daddy said, finishing the quote and also getting up. "All right, but in this age of science, I think somebody should be able to come up with an explanation that doesn't sound straight from voodoo."

"Who's Horatio?" Marian asked.

"A friend of Hamlet's," Ingrid said. "If you read the play you'll know what the quote is about."

"That's schoolwork," Liza said in a loud voice. "This is vacation."

"And what are you two going to do?" Ingrid said. "Why don't you come out with your father and me?"

"Okay," Marian said with a big grin.

Liza sighed romantically. "I thought you'd never ask."

"Morgan and I are going for a walk," I said, and added quickly, "Down by the beach by the trees there, and maybe play ball and build a sandcastle."

"I was hoping you'd make friends with some of the other young people your age," Daddy said.

I wanted to say, And what would happen to Morgan? But I decided not to. He'd probably say that Morgan would do better with his own age group if he didn't have me, and I wondered for a moment if that were right. Then I remembered his face and the way he flung himself at me when I came home from school. So I didn't say anything.

"You'd probably better take your sweaters," Ingrid said. "It's getting chilly."

The light was on when we reached the house in the woods.

"Hi," I said, going in. I wondered about saying her name, which I knew now was Elissa, but decided I wouldn't. "We missed you the other day. And we turned on your light, so what kind of batteries do you use? I'll bring you some more. And Morgan used your charcoal. I hope it's okay."

"Of course. This light takes four D batteries, but I have plenty here. And of course it's all right for Morgan to use the charcoal. What did you do?"

Morgan ran over, pulled his drawings out from her drawing pad and handed them to her.

"That's nice," she said. "But I like your paintings better. Didn't you do any?"

He shook his head and looked at me. "I told him not to. Since you weren't here I didn't think we ought to use your paints. I wasn't sure how we would leave the paint box afterwards."

"Well, come over here sometime this afternoon and I'll show you. Here, Morgan, here are some colors for you and your brush." And she put a lot of colors on a sort of enamel tray and handed it over with the big paint-brush. Then she tipped some of her paint water into a small glass and gave him that.

Morgan came and put his hand on her arm for a moment and smiled. Then he took the tray and the glass and went back to his place on the floor under another light behind the kittens and started sloshing the water around in the paints.

For a moment I wished he would leave so I could talk to the woman about him. I was standing beside her when she looked up at me. "And what would you like to do?"

"I think I'd like to draw the kittens for a while."

She handed me several sheets of paper, the big cardboard and a piece of charcoal. "No paints?"

"No. Not for now."

I'd really planned to go upstairs and walk around and

explore some more, but I decided to work on a drawing of the kittens.

They were clustered around the cat, who was licking them slowly and methodically. Every now and then she'd put out her paw, hold whatever kitten it was down, and when it showed signs of wanting to wiggle away, hold it even more firmly.

"She takes a lot of trouble," I said.

"Yes, she's a good mother."

"Aren't all cats good mothers?"

"For the most part. Occasionally there'll be a cat who abandons her kitten or kittens, but it's rare."

"Unlike humans!" The words were out of my mouth before I even knew I was thinking them.

She painted for a few seconds, then she said, "You say that with a lot of feeling. You think of yourself as abandoned, don't you?"

"Yes. I told you. I'm adopted. My own mother, whoever she was, abandoned me."

"We've talked about this before, and I know I said that she could have done it because it was the best thing for you."

"That's what everybody always says."

"Have you talked with a lot of people about this?"

"No. But I've read books."

"And you think your father is sorry they adopted you?"

"Yes."

I waited for her to say something. But she didn't, and I felt a little disappointed. After a minute something made me say, "Somebody said you went to art school and wanted to be an artist. Is that true?"

"Yes. That was the original plan."

"What made you change your mind?"

"Life, I guess, is the best answer. My older brother, who was going to manage our parents' horse farm, died.

My father is dead, too. My mother is pretty competent to manage the farm, but she can't do it entirely alone. So I decided to help her.''

"That's where you hurt your foot," I said.

"Yes. A horse beside me reared up. So did mine, then took off and I was thrown." She sighed. "It could have been a lot worse. And anyway, it was my own fault. I should never have let such a new rider up on Gypsy. But at the time, she—er—led me to believe that she had had more experience than it turned out she had. I shouldn't have believed the girl, but taken her out instead on somebody like Prince, who is the gentlest horse on earth. The trouble is, he's not the most exciting ride going and I somehow got the idea that the girl wanted a challenging ride and she was testing out horse farms to see how we all did. More fool me!'' She glanced down at me. "Where did you get all this gossip? Or shouldn't I ask?''

"The Brintons. They took Daddy and Ingrid and the twins and a couple of other people out in their boat and then came to lunch.''

"I see." She dabbed her paintbrush into her water. "Any other fascinating things come to light?''

I knew I shouldn't have brought any of it up. But I had, so I said, "Dr. Brinton said something about a scandal and Mrs. Brinton sort of shut him up.''

"I'll bet she did.''

I looked up at her. "You don't like her?''

"I like her all right, and she's a good customer. She's also a good rider. But—well, in a small community like this, I guess gossip is inevitable.''

I waited for her to go on. When she didn't I wondered if I had the nerve to ask her straight out what the scandal was, but knew I didn't, even though she was one of the nicest adults I'd ever met and until this moment I'd have sworn I could have asked her anything.

"I suppose you want to know what the scandal was."

"Only if you want to tell me," I said virtuously.

She turned around and laughed. "You're a bad liar, Bridget, so I strongly urge you not to take up a life of crime."

I grinned rather feebly.

She sighed. "I ran away with a married man from around here. It wasn't the wisest or best thing I ever did, from any standpoint, including my own. I could not have been more wrong about anyone, but that's only one of the things that was wrong with it. Anyway, he went back to his wife. So that was the end of that."

I thought about it for a moment. In a way it sounded romantic, but I knew it hadn't been. "I guess you felt abandoned," I said.

She laughed in a voice that cracked a little and put her hand up to her face. "I guess you could say I did."

To my great surprise I got up and went over to her and gave her a hug. I'd really never done this to anyone since Mother died, but I knew she wouldn't push me away or think what a creep I was.

She put her arm out around me and hugged me back and rested her head against me for a moment. "You're nice, Bridget. Very nice. Did anyone ever tell you that?"

"No," I said.

After that I drew for a while and then went upstairs, wondering if I'd have the same sensation of pressing against a wall when I tried to walk in the hall and the rooms.

It was there, but not as much. I had a weird feeling

that the ghosts of the people who'd lived there had become used to me and decided I was okay.

I wandered into the room with the desk and pulled open the flap with another huge puff of dust. After several sneezes I found myself looking at the cubbyholes with the greenish paper sticking out. Without thinking, I pulled out one of the pieces of paper. It almost came apart. Handling it as carefully as I could, I opened it up. Obviously it was a letter; I could see that even though it was upside down. I turned it right way up. Most of the page was blurred, as though water had dripped on it. Only a couple of lines were readable. There was no date, just crooked handwriting that looked wavery. "My darling wife" was the salutation. "I am now convinced that soon you're going to leave me and find I cannot bear the thought. I have decided that it would be much better if we were both dead."

—10—

A chill went through me as I reread the words. I stared at them, then tried to go through the rest of the letter to see if I could make out any of the other words. But there were holes in the paper, as though something had eaten it. Half the name of the person to whom it was addressed was gone, and what was left was blurred. I bent forward to try and catch the light from the window. Then I picked up the paper, got up and was about to walk to the window when half of it fell to the floor.

I put it back on the desk flap as carefully as I could. Then I sat down and stared at it again. After turning my head this way and that—I didn't dare touch the paper again—I made out what I thought were three words: ". . . been a bad husb . . ." There was another blur after the *b*. After a little more staring and turning my head I decided the whole sentence must be, "I know I've been a bad husband."

Gingerly, gently, I pulled out some of the other papers. Bits of them fell onto the desk flap and dust filled the air. I sneezed, blowing the papers back against the pigeonholes, and then sneezed three times more. Frantically I searched for a tissue in my pockets and finally found one. As carefully as I could, I turned some of the papers over to see if they were all

87

letters. I decided some of them were, but some were either not letters or were middle pages of long letters, with no salutation or ending. For the next hour or so I sat at the desk, screwing my head around to see if I could read any of the words on any of the six or seven sheets of paper. At the end of an hour I'd been able to put a few sentences together, but not so they made any real sense, and it was getting even harder to see. I had no idea what time it was, but it was obvious that the sun had changed position because the room was suddenly fairly dark.

I went to the window and tried to see out of it, past the dirt and the cobwebs. One thing was obvious: it was raining, and as I listened I could hear the sound of distant thunder. I knew that I should go downstairs and collect Morgan and go home for lunch. But I continued standing there. There was a sofa in the room, back against the wall with all the books. Without thinking, I went over and sat down on it. Clouds of dust arose, and I could hear small feet scurrying. But none of it seemed to matter. My eyelids were like lead. I lay down and went to sleep.

I didn't know where I was, but I was very happy. I was swimming in water that was a turquoise blue, like the sky. A great sense of peace and contentment filled me. I even felt exalted in some strange way, as though something or someone, without speaking, had sent happiness flooding through me, and it was a good omen. . . .

Breaking into that was a man's voice talking. He sounded angry. Then he was yelling. I couldn't make out the words, but he was beside himself with rage. I heard another voice, a woman's, pleading. She began to cry. Her voice rose higher. There was an awful sound. I started screaming. . . .

"Maybe you shouldn't take a nap up here," Elissa said. She was sitting on the couch beside me. She was smiling, but she also looked anxious.

I sat up. "I was dreaming," I said. My head felt strange.

"I'd have guessed that. What did you dream?"

"At first I was tremendously happy. I was in very blue water, swimming. It was warm and I felt absolutely—well, happy hardly describes it. It was as though . . . as though everything was going to be happy forever. Then . . . all of a sudden there was a man's voice, yelling and angry, and a woman's sort of pleading and then she began to cry. And there was some kind of horrible sound and I started to scream. I guess that was what you heard." At that point I looked up at Elissa and saw Morgan behind her. "Hi, Morgan."

He came around Elissa and touched my leg.

"Sorry about the fuss," I said, embarrassed. We were all silent for a moment, then I asked Elissa, "Do you know who used to live here?"

"No. I've been away except for the past three years. The only thing I've heard is that it was some kind of summer home."

"What a weird place to have it—in the woods like this. I mean, it's the middle of nowhere!"

"I have a feeling that some of the trees aren't that old. It could have had no trees in front of it, or just a sprinkling. All that we see now could have sprung up since."

"But who'd leave a place looking like this? I mean, it's filthy and all that. But some of the furniture might have been nice—once."

"I've sort of wondered, too. I did ask Mother, but she hasn't been here that long. Dad only bought the horse farm about eleven or twelve years ago. We used to live outside New London. I'll ask her." She got up. "I enjoy your company, yours and Morgan's, but I feel bound to ask you if you were due home for lunch."

At that moment, a great clap of thunder sounded almost overhead. I don't like thunder and I hate lightning. Neither does Morgan. "We can't go home in this," I said.

"No, I suppose you can't. I hadn't realized it was that close. I brought a sandwich and a soda, which I'll be glad to share."

But, for once in my life, I didn't feel hungry. "Maybe Morgan would like some, but I'm not hungry. Thanks anyway. Morgan—" But he seemed to have vanished. Then I saw him at the desk flap, his hand out.

"Don't touch those!" I yelled.

He whirled around, scowling.

"Sorry. I didn't mean to yell at you, but those pieces of paper are practically falling apart. I've been trying to read them without touching them."

Slowly Morgan put his hand down. His scowl lightened.

"What are they?" Elissa asked. She picked up her cane and limped over to the desk. "Good heavens! They look like letters." She glanced up at the back of the desk. "Did you get them from the pigeonholes?"

"Yes. I mean, they were just left. Anybody could have read them."

She looked back at me and smiled. "I didn't mean to suggest you'd done anything wrong." Reaching out her hand, she touched some of the papers that were still in the holes. "I see what you mean about their falling apart." She glanced down at the papers spread out on the desk flap and stood, turning her head as I'd done.

Slowly I walked over to where she was standing and stood beside her, looking down at the paper.

I pointed to the words and read out, " 'been a bad husband.' At least, I think that's what it says."

"I think you're right. How fascinating!"

"The trouble is, when I try to look at some of the others, they fall apart. I'm afraid to touch them."

"Yes. I'm afraid they're rotted with years and dust and mildew." She looked at some of the blurred words. "Not to mention water. But maybe we can work at them a little, if we're careful." She glanced at me. "Would you like to?"

"Yes," I said, surprised how much I wanted to. "I'd like to a lot."

"Maybe if we put a sheet or cloth on top of those that are out now it might help preserve them. Morgan, I have a cotton jacket downstairs. Do you think you could bring it up here?"

He nodded and flew out the door.

He was so different here in the house with Elissa, I thought, and burst out, "I wish he could be with you more. I wish we both could." I wasn't used to making sudden declarations like that and felt shy. Whenever I'd liked anybody and said so, and it got around, I was teased. "Don't tell a—" I started, meaning don't tell anybody. But it sounded so idiotic.

"I won't tell anybody," she said. "Why should I? And I wish I could be with you and Morgan, too. I'm glad you feel the way you do."

Morgan came back in with the jacket. Elissa laid it flat across the papers on the desk flap. "That's the best I can do right now. I have a friend in Boston who deals with old documents, so I'll call him up and see if he has any suggestions. Let's go downstairs."

* * *

The storm raged for another hour. Elissa and Morgan painted. I tried to draw the cat and thought about the letters upstairs. In some weird way I felt terribly close to them, but I couldn't quite figure out how. Suddenly I said, "Will you be able to talk to that man, the one in Boston, soon?"

"I can try over the weekend. If he's there, then I can."

"I wish he was here."

"Why are you in such a hurry?"

"I don't know," I said after a minute. "I just am."

"What's happening with your family? What are they doing while you're here?"

I shrugged. "Going out on the boat. Having picnics. Playing tennis at the club or talking to the people down on the beach."

"Don't you ever go out with them?"

"No," I said. "Not if we can help it."

There was another silence. Then she said, "It's beginning to clear up. Hadn't you better be getting back?"

"Yes. I suppose so," I said. What I really wanted to do was to go back upstairs and look at more letters. I wanted to understand the connection I felt to them.

"Just as a matter of curiosity, what do you tell them when you and Morgan come here?"

Morgan looked at me rather anxiously. I wondered if he worried about Elissa making us tell Daddy and Ingrid the truth, or maybe telling them herself.

"She wouldn't," I said without thinking, as though Morgan had spoken.

"Who wouldn't what?" Elissa asked.

I hesitated. I realized my ability to know what Morgan was thinking was considered spooky by some people and unhealthy by others. But I was pretty sure she'd understand. "I usually say Morgan and I walk in the woods by the lakeshore. And when I said 'She wouldn't,' I meant you. I knew Morgan was worrying that if I told you what we said when we came here you might make us tell the truth—about coming to the house. But I said you wouldn't.''

"No, I wouldn't. But I do think it's better if you don't have to lie. Makes things much less complicated." She looked up at me for a moment. "You don't like sailing, and you don't much like playing around the beach, I take it. Is there anything else you do like to do?"

"In our last summer house we could walk to town and could go and look at bookstores and things. Here, either you sail or play on the beach or go with the others."

"Ye-es." She painted for a while. Then she said, "Have you ever ridden? On a horse?"

"No," I said.

Morgan shook his head.

"You might try it. I'm bound to say that exercise is not a bad thing for you, and you don't seem to me to get much."

Of course I felt instantly that she was talking about my pudginess and froze.

She glanced at my face. "No, Bridget, I'm not talking about your figure any more than I'm talking about Morgan's. Exercise is good for everyone, short, tall, thin, fat and everything in between."

I saw a movement out of the corner of my eye and saw Morgan nodding.

"Morgan seems to think it's a good idea, too," I said. "But doesn't it cost a lot of money?"

"Oh—" She painted a few strokes. "Sometimes yes, sometimes no. Why don't you come by the farm tomorrow morning. You can see it from your house, I think, and can walk there quite easily."

"And then we can say we're riding when we're really here," I said.

"Well, not quite. But at least you can report on another activity. That ought to keep some nagging away. The sun seems to be trying to come out now, so maybe you'd better get back. Come by the farm tomorrow morning!"

The next morning Morgan came to my room and tugged on my pillow before I was even awake. When I looked up I saw he was fully dressed. Then he pointed towards the window. Slowly I got out of bed and went to the window. Some distance away and on the other side of the road, I saw horses in a meadow. They must have been there other mornings, but I'd never noticed.

"You want to go look at the horses?" I asked sleepily.

He nodded.

I showered and got dressed and was downstairs with Morgan for breakfast before Daddy and the twins were up. When Ingrid asked where we were going, I said, "Down to the beach," and then we got out before she had a chance to reply.

We did indeed go to the beach but went from there almost immediately back to the road.

When we reached the horse farm we stood at the gate for a while looking at the horses in the paddock. There was a big black one, a smaller chestnut and a couple of what looked like plain brown ones. Then there trotted through a gate on the far side a sort of dappled brown and white pony with a long mane and tail and a nose he kept pointing in the air. I watched them because they were beautiful and I like animals, but my mind was on the letters in the haunted house. I felt an urgency about them, as though there were a message there for me. That seemed so weird that

I told myself it was nonsense. But I couldn't stop thinking about them.

Suddenly Morgan looked at me and pointed straight at the pony. Then he was over the fence and tearing across the paddock before I could even move.

"Morgan, come back!" I yelled.

But he went straight on running till he got to the pony. When he was about ten feet from it he stopped. I was trying to get there and to remember at the same time whether Morgan had ever been around any horses. Not when I was with him, I thought, but I hadn't been with him all the time. One of his many nannies might have taken him to see horses.

"Morgan," I called out.

He was walking slowly now towards the pony, whose head was up, looking at him.

"Mor—" I started again.

He turned and put his fingers to his lips and scowled.

"But he could bite you!"

He shook his head. Then, with his hand out, he walked even more slowly forward towards the pony.

I knew I ought to stop him, that the pony could bite him or rear up and trample him, but I didn't do anything. Something about the way Morgan was doing this, as though he'd done it before and knew how, kept me still.

Then Morgan was up to the pony, still holding out his hand. Finally, with the same hand, he patted the pony's neck, and made odd noises while he was doing it, sounds I'd never heard from him before.

The pony didn't seem to mind. After a while it dipped its nose into his hand.

"He and the pony seem to have struck up a friendship," Elissa's voice said from the side, and I saw her coming towards us, limping but not with a cane.

"I never thought he'd been near a horse," I said.

"Either he has, or he has some instinct for them, because he knows how to approach one. Morgan, that's Tomboy. He seems to like you."

Morgan nodded, then put his hand up on the pony's back and looked at her.

"You want to ride?" she asked.

He nodded.

"All right. Then take hold of his bridle like this—" and she slid two fingers under the bridle around Tomboy's chin—"and see if you can lead him back to the barn. I can put a saddle on him there."

I thought the pony would protest, but he didn't. Morgan put a hand up and slid his fingers under the bridle the way Elissa had demonstrated and proceeded to follow Elissa. Wondering if the pony were really that obedient or whether he wanted to go back anyway, I followed the three of them.

It was a big barn with stalls for horses, all of them now empty. Elissa took a saddle off some kind of holder on the wall and came towards the pony. She put it on his back, buckling the straps under his stomach.

"All right, now, Morgan. Come here. On this side here, put your right foot in the stirrup and throw the other leg over."

I couldn't believe how easily he did it.

"Have you done that before, Morgan?" I asked.

He acted as though he hadn't heard me.

"What about you, Bridget?" Elissa asked.

I had on jeans, of course, and a T-shirt, but all I could think of was the things I'd heard about how well people looked in the saddle—thin people.

"I'll look like an idiot," I said.

"No you won't. I'm going to saddle Belinda for you. She's gentle and has a nice personality—like you!"

I could feel myself blushing.

Elissa had disappeared, but she reappeared leading a light chestnut horse with an even lighter mane and tail.

I watched while she put a saddle on and buckled it. "Now," Elissa said. "Come over here on this side, put your right foot in the stirrup and fling your other leg over."

I did as she said and for the first time in my life found myself sitting on top of a horse.

For the next hour or so Elissa stood in the middle of the paddock and told Morgan and me the basic elements of walking, trotting, cantering, what to do with our legs and hands and what not to do.

It was fun. I liked Belinda, who responded to my heels when I touched them to her sides and to any pressure of my hands on the reins.

"Bridget, you're very good. You seem to have a natural feel for riding. Morgan, you're good, too, but not when you act as though this were the Derby and you were going to win it. Now I think that's enough for both of you this first time or you'll be so sore you won't be able to sit down."

I saw Morgan scowl. "Come on, Morgan," I said.

"Yes. You can come back tomorrow," Elissa agreed. "Bring your horses back to the barn where you can unsaddle them."

A fraction of a moment before she finished speaking I saw a familiar set look on Morgan's face and knew he was not going to do what she said. "Mor—" I began.

But it was too late. He pushed his heels into Tomboy's sides and took off across the paddock.

"Morgan!" Elissa called.

Tomboy ran around the field and then just as I yelled "No!" gathered his legs under him and jumped the fence. I expected Morgan to come off, but by some miracle he didn't.

"Oh my God!" Elissa said. Then she turned to me. "Get off, Bridget. I'm going to have to go after him."

"Maybe I could—"

"No. Now get off quickly!"

So I did, and stood there in the middle of the field as she quickly swung herself into the saddle, then galloped towards the same part of the fence that Morgan had jumped over and leaped it.

—11—

It seemed a long time but probably wasn't before I heard the sound of horses' hooves again and saw Elissa approaching on Belinda and leading Tomboy by his rein.

"Can you open the gate for us, Bridget?"

I ran forward and slid the latch up on the gate and pulled it open. Elissa went through, followed by Morgan on Tomboy. Morgan's face had an angry, stubborn expression.

I followed them to the barn and held Belinda while Elissa went over to Morgan.

"Get down, Morgan," she said quietly. It was amazing, I thought. She'd always seemed so gentle to me, but this was a voice I wouldn't have disobeyed. For a moment I held my breath. Then he got down.

"Now listen to me, Morgan. I know you have certain frustrations, and I sympathize. But don't ever, ever do that again. It's a miracle you didn't come off when Tomboy went over that fence. If you had, who do you think would have been blamed? Look at me!"

Morgan had been staring at the floor, but at that he quickly looked up.

"Number one, you're very good on a horse, but you're not yet an experienced rider, and you could have caused Tomboy to break a leg. If that happened he'd have to be shot! Number two, you could have hurt your-

99

self and I would have had to bear the responsibility for it with your father. He could sue the whole farm from under us.''

Morgan's face crumpled, his eyes filled and he started to cry.

''All right. I don't like scolding you, but you mustn't do that again. You have to promise me, or I won't let you ride one of my horses. Is that understood?''

Morgan nodded vigorously, then surprised me by putting his arms around her waist.

''Yes, I like you very much, too.'' She looked at me. ''As I do Bridget. But I also like my horses and my farm.''

We helped Elissa remove the saddles and put them away and she showed us how to brush the horses. Then she let them back out into the field.

''Bridget,'' she said as we were about to go, ''you really do ride well. I wasn't just saying that. I think you should take it up.'' She smiled. ''And you look very good in the saddle!''

All the way back to the cottage I thought about telling Daddy and Ingrid and the others that Morgan and I had been riding. After all, that was one of the reasons we'd gone there, so we'd have something we could say we'd been doing. So why was I afraid to?

Because Ingrid might find something wrong with it, and if she did, then Daddy would, too?

Because they'd maybe want to know how we'd met Elissa? And then they'd learn about the house in the woods?

Because they'd want to come and see us ride, and despite everything Elissa had said, I'd look awful or make a fool of myself or both and the twins would tease me?

Because if Ingrid got to know about the house in the

woods, she might—horror of horrors—insist on visiting it?

"Do you think we ought to tell them about us riding?" I asked Morgan.

The violent shake of his head reassured me. "No, I don't think so either."

Luckily, when we got back to lunch nobody asked what we'd been doing. Linda and Steve were there, and there was a lot of talk about the tennis games they'd played and a quick trip out in the boat for Steve, the twins and Daddy. Daddy, Ingrid and the twins were going out on the Brintons' boat after lunch and they talked about that, too.

Then, just as we were all about to get up, Ingrid said to me, "Did you and Morgan have a nice walk?"

"Yes, thanks."

Daddy looked first at me and then at Morgan. For a moment I thought he might say something, but he didn't.

Morgan and I slipped out while they were getting stuff ready for the Brintons' trip. We knew the way through the woods to the house so well now it was almost as though there were a path.

When we got there, Morgan went straight to the paints Elissa had left for him and I went upstairs to the desk.

Elissa's jacket was still over the desk flap. I lifted it as carefully as I could and started trying again to make out some of the writing on the pages. By this time I'd learned how to touch them and move them gently so they didn't come apart as easily as before.

A lot of the writing was too blurred to read, but I could figure out more this time, bits of sentences: ". . . been a bad husband and you . . . a bad wife . . . the baby is too young to know . . . I am afraid for her." Then the names Boston and New York. Then, "The

101

baby is wonderful . . . but she keeps crying . . . not my fault . . . lawyers . . ."

I was in the middle of trying to decipher this when I suddenly felt a hand on my shoulder and let out a yell.

"Sorry. I didn't mean to frighten you," Elissa said.

"It's okay."

"Found anything new?"

I showed her the bits I'd been able to read. "I was thinking, should I write down what I can read in a notebook or something?"

"That'd probably be a good idea, because I don't know how much will remain readable once we move the pieces."

I pulled a small notebook out of my jeans pocket and a ballpoint out of the other. "I brought these along." Then I said, "Were you able to talk to the man who knows about old documents?"

"No, unfortunately not. He's away on business. We'll just have to move them as carefully as we can."

She had been leaning over me looking at the papers, but she straightened up. "Well, good luck."

When she left I went back to the pages. Maybe because I had become used to the handwriting, or maybe because a little success had cheered me on, I was able to make out even more than earlier that afternoon, and I wrote all the words down, indicating whether they were separate or came in sentences.

After a while I'd finished with all the pages that were out. Touching and lifting them as carefully as I could, I put them on a table nearby, to stay there until I was ready to close the flap and could put them in one of the drawers or somewhere else safe.

Then I pulled more pages out of the cubbyholes. Some of them I saw right away were in different handwriting. The first writing was slanted to the right. This was straight up and down, but the pages were just as fragile as the first batch, and I still could get only isolated words and sentences.

I worked for what seemed a long time, filling page after page of my notebook.

Then, all of a sudden, I was so sleepy I could barely sit in the chair. Pushing the chair back, I went over to the sofa and lay down. The next thing I knew, I was asleep.

It was the same dream I'd had before, and in a weird way, I knew I was dreaming. There was the feeling of total happiness, of being absolutely safe and loved, then the voices of a man and a woman, and the shouts and, once again, I was screaming.

"Maybe you should avoid the sofa," Elissa said.

I sat up. "Did I make a noise again?"

"I'm afraid so. How do you feel?"

And then out of my mouth came words I never even thought of before. "I've been here before."

"You mean before two or three weeks ago?"

"Yes."

There was a silence. Then she surprised me. "I've wondered about that."

"Why?"

"I'm not sure. But it has crossed my mind." We sat there for a moment, then she said, "Bridget, what do you think of our going to the town hall or wherever they keep their civic records and seeing who lived in this house before, and, if possible, who owns it now?"

"Yes, yes, let's! That's a wonderful idea!"

The problem was how to get there without being found out. I still thought of Elissa as my own secret.

She looked down at me. "You haven't told your father about me, have you?"

"No. How did you know?"

"Well, you haven't told them about your coming here, have you, and the house and I sort of go together."

103

She paused. "I was going to speak to you about telling your father about riding at the farm. I have to insist
that you do that. He could very rightly criticize me if I
let you ride without his knowledge and permission."

For a moment I was angry. Then I realized she was
right. And she'd been wonderfully kind to me. "All
right. I don't know what he'll say, but I'll tell him, and
I'll come to the farm tomorrow morning."

Before I left I put Elissa's jacket over the papers on the
table and some ordinary sheets of paper from my notebook over those on the desk flap.

The next morning I sat at breakfast munching my
cereal and wondering how to bring up the subject of my
riding. Ingrid and the twins had gone somewhere and
Daddy was reading his copy of the *New York Times*.
Morgan arrived downstairs and slid into his chair at the
table. I'd told him the previous evening that I was going
to go to the stable and asked him if he wanted to come.
He nodded, but not as enthusiastically as usual, and I
wondered if Elissa's scolding the previous day had made
him angry. More even than most kids his age, Morgan
did not like to be told what to do, how to do it or when.
True, he'd hugged her, but one of the things I'd discovered about Morgan is that he could feel two things at
once.

And then the totally unexpected happened. Daddy
looked up straight at Morgan, smiled and said, "I'm
taking the boat out this morning by myself. Would you
like to come?"

I couldn't believe it when Morgan nodded. I stared
at him. He did not stare back. In fact, he attacked his
cereal with concentration.

"Fine," Daddy said, getting up. "Come on out to
the beach and let's get started."

As I watched them go, part of me was angry that not

only had Daddy not invited me, he hadn't even looked at me, and part was relieved that I hadn't had a chance to tell him about the stable. As I finished my cereal I wondered whether Daddy had spoken to Morgan about going out on the boat the night before when I wasn't around. Or maybe it was because it was the first time Daddy asked Morgan by himself, so that there'd just be the two of them. Whatever the reason, I decided to be grateful.

Half an hour later I walked down the main road towards the horse farm and watched the horses frolicking around the paddock. One of the cars that passed me going back towards our house was ours, with Ingrid and the twins in it. I saw Ingrid's startled look and then the twins' faces through the back window as they turned and stared after me. Something made me wave.

"All right," Elissa said when I got to the barn, "get Belinda's bridle and saddle and I'll show you how to put them on her."

As I followed her step-by-step instructions, she explained what purpose each served. When Belinda was ready Elissa said, "I'm going out with you this morning. My foot is pretty much healed and I don't have to coddle it anymore."

She was riding the big black horse I'd seen last time. "What's his name?" I asked.

"Stafford. He's large and occasionally willful, but on the whole he's my favorite ride. Keep your elbows down, Bridget, and your back straight. Now come along out here to the ring for some basic lessons."

The ring was at the back of the barn and once there I walked, stopped, trotted, stopped and cantered and stopped, all the while learning about rising in the saddle every other step Belinda took.

"No, don't pull on her mouth. It's very sensitive, and it's through her mouth that you tell her mostly what you want her to do. And use your heels! Like this! Don't rise too high; there shouldn't be too much space between your bottom and your saddle. You're catching on nicely!"

At the end of the hour we went for a ride down a lane behind the barn and through some of the fields. I loved it. I found I wasn't afraid or nervous on Belinda, something I always thought I would be, and even though this was only the second time I'd ridden and the second time I'd been on her, I felt she and I understood each other.

"I think Belinda's wonderful!" I said.

"She is. She's a sweet horse."

"She has a beautiful soul."

Elissa grinned. "I agree." Then, as we neared the barn, "I was sort of surprised that Morgan didn't come with you."

"So was I. And I was almost knocked flat when Daddy invited him to go for a sail and he accepted. I didn't think he liked sailing. He always shook his head before when Daddy or Ingrid or the twins tried to get him to go."

"Does anybody have any idea why he doesn't talk? Is there any physical basis for it?"

"None. At least none that all the hordes of doctors have discovered." I paused and then burst out, "I'm always afraid that somebody—some doctor or expert— will say he ought to be in a hospital or institution. I think Daddy's been talking to Dr. Brinton about it."

Elissa didn't say anything for a moment. Then, "It must be frustrating for your father, especially as there seems to be nothing physically wrong. I'm glad they're out sailing together. I don't suppose you have any idea what might have happened—about his not talking, I mean—if the problem is psychological."

"No. Mother died, of course, when he was two, and I don't remember if he said anything before that, al-

106

though if he had I'm sure somebody would have remembered. Do you think it's because she died?''

''Possibly, but by no means necessarily. I've read muteness can be caused by some kind of trauma, but I don't know any more than that. By the way, did you speak—''

''No,'' I forestalled her quickly. ''I'm sorry, I meant to. I was trying to decide how to start when Morgan came down and Daddy asked him to go sailing. But I will!''

''I'm sure you will. Now, if we're going to go into town we'd better get back to the barn.''

There were several people saddling and unsaddling horses in and just outside the barn as we returned.

''Hi! Bridget!'' somebody said, and there was Steve.
''Oh, hi.''
''I didn't know you rode.''
''I've just begun.'' I got down off the horse and realized I'd better have that talk with Daddy as soon as I got home. Steve would tell Linda and Linda would be sure to bring it up at one of the picnics or barbecues.

''Do you like it?'' Steve swung himself off his horse and started unbuckling the girth straps.

''Yes. It's fun.''
''Maybe we could go for a ride sometime.''
''Doesn't Linda ride?''
''As a matter of fact, no. But even if she did, there's no reason why we shouldn't, is there?''
''No.''
''Ready?'' Elissa said, standing at the door of the stall.

''Yes.'' As I passed Steve, still grooming his horse, I waved.

''Why are you looking so grumpy?'' Elissa asked, as we got into her car on the other side of the yard.

''He asked me if we couldn't ride sometime.''

107

"Why should that upset you? He seems like a nice boy."

"His girl friend is Linda. She's smashingly pretty."

"And you're a nice-looking girl, too, Bridget. Yes, I know, you have a thing about your weight. First of all, it's not that bad. Second, you have a very pretty face, and third, tastes differ."

"You should hear Daddy and Ingrid and the twins on the subject."

"It's a shame, because I think it's warping you in your response to people. It makes it hard to like somebody, you know, if she acts like a surly bear when you say something nice."

"I suppose so." I didn't want to think about maybe Steve liking me. It's so horribly easy to be let down.

The office of records was in the back of the little town hall. Elissa did most of the talking.

"We were just interested in who might have owned the house before and who might own it now."

The clerk went off for a while and then came back. "It seems to have been owned by a Patrick Bingham, who used it as a summer residence. The rest of the year he lived in Connecticut."

The name sent a little shiver down my arm.

"Does he still own it?" Elissa asked.

"I guess he must. It doesn't seem to belong to anyone else."

"Is there an address for him?" I asked.

"Doesn't seem to be."

"How long has it been unoccupied?" It was such an ordinary question, but I could feel my heart pounding.

"Far as I can make out from this, about twelve years."

—12—

I stared back at the man. Twelve years ago I would have been two.

"Thanks a lot," Elissa said.

We went outside and stood on the sidewalk. "Patrick Bingham," I said.

"Does it ring any bell?"

I paused. "Not exactly. Not a real memory. But when I heard the name I felt . . . well, almost like I'd known it before."

Elissa said gently, "Just relax. I'm sure if there's something there it will come back to you."

We started walking back towards the car. I was so busy trying to think and trying to remember that I wasn't looking where I was going and almost walked into Daddy and Morgan.

"Well, hello!" Daddy said.

Startled, I looked up. For a few seconds we stood there until I suddenly realized that Daddy didn't know who Elissa was. "Er, this is my father, Elissa. Daddy, this is Elissa."

"How do you do," Daddy said.

Morgan made a sound, and, looking at him, I saw his face was rigid with fright. As though I could read his mind I knew he was terrified that either Elissa or I would tell Daddy about the house in the woods. He needn't have worried. I didn't want Daddy to know about the house any more than Morgan did.

Elissa smiled and said, "I'm Elissa Hamilton. Mother and I have the horse farm down the road from where you're staying. Bridget and I have been riding."

"Riding!" Daddy couldn't have looked more amazed if she had said plane gliding.

"Yes, and Bridget seems to have a natural feel for it. Considering her inexperience, she handles the horse very well."

"I didn't know you were riding, Bridget," Daddy said.

"I was going to tell you this morning," I put in quickly, "because Elissa said I must yesterday."

"I see."

"I thought you'd be pleased," I said, not quite truthfully. He often didn't like things he hadn't thought of himself—at least at first.

"Well, I certainly think you could use some exercise. As I've said—"

"Don't!" I blurted out. "Please don't."

"Don't what?" He was indignant.

"Don't say what you were going to say. Not here."

"And what was I going to say?"

If I hadn't known before, I knew now why keeping the secret of the old house and Elissa had been so important. When I was with the family I was one person: overweight- Bridget-who-was-adopted-and-who-needed-to-exercise-and-had-to-watch-her-diet. In the old house with Elissa I was just myself, Bridget. I knew I couldn't bear to have the two pushed together in front of Elissa. But I also knew that that was what Daddy was about to do. So I ran. I ran in the only direction there was to run, across the road.

I was aware of the shrieking of brakes and the front of a car almost under my nose, but I didn't get hit. There

110

were shouts and slamming doors, but I kept on running until I got to the mall. Then I ducked into the bookstore and hid behind one of the display shelves.

I stayed there for what felt like a long time, numbly reading and rereading the titles of the mysteries and science fiction paperback novels.

What was going to happen now?

I'd never run away from any of them like this before. Daddy and Ingrid, when she heard about it, would be furious. I'd have to endure lecture after lecture about my inconsiderate behavior, my "surly emotionalism," my tendency to take everything personally, my inability to get along with others, how different I was from the twins, and so on and so on, with a side trip into how much better I'd be if I could just control my eating, like Liza, and Marian.

And Morgan?

In all of this I hadn't thought about Morgan. Now I did. Where would he be and how would he make out with the others if I weren't there? Maybe better, my present depressed state answered. And just having the question in my mind made me realize that I was thinking of keeping on running. Where to? To whom?

I thought then of Elissa.

But Elissa would by now have been brainwashed with the family version of Bridget.

Nobody was around, so I sat down on the floor and started to cry.

"Hi. What seems to be the matter?"

I looked up. It was Steve. He squatted down beside me. "What's the matter, Bridget?"

"Why aren't you with Linda?" I asked, crying.

"Why do you always drag Linda into everything I say?"

111

"Because she's thin and beautiful and I can't figure out why you're even talking to me."

There was a pause. "I guess because there's something about you that gets to me. Sort of like a puppy I once had that had been abused."

"That's great. A dog! Thanks a lot!"

I didn't want to cry with him there, but I couldn't stop and I was afraid that Daddy or Ingrid and the twins or even Elissa might be outside.

After a while he said, "What are you going to do?"

"I don't know."

What I wanted to do, I suddenly knew, was to go back to the house in the woods, to go on looking through the letters and the papers, to see what I could find out about Patrick Bingham and the house and his wife and the baby mentioned in the letters. As I thought of his name I felt again that movement, like a stirring of air, over my skin.

Slowly I got to my feet, helped a little by Steve. His hand was still holding my arm when he said, "I wish you wouldn't keep putting yourself down the way you do. You have a lot going for you."

I opened my mouth, but before I could say anything, he shook my arm and said, "And don't go dragging Linda in again."

I thought about the boy I'd seen with Linda in the back of the car and it was almost more than I could do not to say anything about it. Instead, I said "Thanks" and went around the bookshelves into the main part of the store.

I couldn't see any of the family around, nor Elissa, and as far as I could make out, none of the cars belonging to any of them was in the parking lot.

Steve, of course, was back in the store, and maybe he'd drive me to the place on the road where I'd turn off to the house in the woods, but then I'd have to explain where I was going. I'd just have to walk.

"Want a lift?"

I turned and looked at Steve. Walking meant five miles. "Okay. Thanks."

We drove for a while. "Are you going to bite my head off or try to get out of the car if I ask you a question?"

"Depends what it is."

"All right. I'll risk it. Why did you run like a bat out of you know what across the road?"

"You saw it, I guess."

"Sure I saw it. Considering the squealing of tires and blowing of horns, there couldn't have been many people around who missed it."

I didn't know how to answer, not without giving away a lot I didn't want to talk about, so I stared into my lap.

"Okay. Let it go."

Finally I said, "Daddy was asking questions."

"Parents can sometimes be the pits."

"Especially when they're not your real parents."

"You know, I've heard him mention you now and again when we've been out on the boat, and he doesn't talk about you any differently from the way he does the others—the twins or Morgan."

"What has he said about me?"

"That you're bright. That your English teacher at school said you were outstandingly good, that he didn't know what he'd do without you when it came to Morgan."

"He's never said a word to me like that!"

"I thought he probably hadn't, which is why I mentioned it."

To my horror I found the tears again in my eyes. I also wanted to blow my nose, so I groped around for a tissue but couldn't find any.

113

"Here," he said, and handed me a medium-clean handkerchief. "It's not as dirty as it looks."

"Thanks."

I blew my nose and wiped my eyes and then wondered if I ought to return it to him. "I guess I'd better keep this and put it in the laundry and give it back to you later."

"All right."

"I always thought he was sorry he and Mother adopted me."

"To tell you the truth, I don't think he even thinks of you in those terms."

"Well, Ingrid certainly does! She's always saying things like 'But I'm talking about your real parents.' And making a big deal as to who they were and what ethnic background they came from."

"Ingrid is a pain in the you know what and she has all the tact of an elephant."

It was so wonderful to hear that, I just sat there for a while and listened. Then I said, "I thought everybody thought she was great!"

"According to my parents, good nannies are hard to find."

"Why should your parents need a nanny? They're both alive, aren't they? We've always had to have one— at least since Mother died. But that's different."

"Yes, but my father's in the Foreign Service, and they've been in posts, especially when we were little, when they needed somebody who was more than just a baby-sitter, because part of their job was to go out a lot and entertain a lot. I've heard Mom and Dad moan over the shortage of good ones."

"Well, Daddy thinks Ingrid's the sun, the moon and the stars!"

"You know, Bridget, your dad is a very bright guy when it comes to things like corporate law and com-

114

puters and political economy, but he's not what I'd call sharp about people. I think he's missed your mom a lot, and wants to do right by you and the other kids, but isn't too sure how.''

''I know you say he talks about how bright I am, but all he does is criticize me, and just sits there when Ingrid goes on about my not being a real daughter, like Liza and Marian.''

''Yeah, I know.''

''How do you know? I haven't told you before.''

''Other people have noticed, too.''

''I don't know what she gets out of it, except to put me down in front of Daddy. I can't help wondering . . .'' I didn't want to even put it into words.

''If she's out to marry your father? I wouldn't be too surprised, except that I think she has a boyfriend somewhere.''

''How do you know?''

''I've been in the post office when she's made long distance calls from the pay phone there. I couldn't hear who she was calling. But she looked happy and kind of lovey-dovey.''

''And she always goes on about . . . well about how I should be on a diet, and it makes me feel like I weigh two hundred pounds.'' I was sorry the minute I said that. It was the last subject in the world I should have brought up.

''Well, you don't look it!''

I glanced at his profile. I couldn't believe he'd said that. ''I don't?''

''No. You're a little on the chubby side, but you'll probably lose that about two or three years down the road. I know you have a thing about it, but you shouldn't!''

I kept staring at him. He was unbelievably good-looking, and he was saying this to me! At that point he turned and smiled at me a little. And then I remembered Linda. I looked down.

"How . . . how did you know how I felt about . . . about the dieting and weight and stuff?"

"Because every time anybody brings up the subject your face shows a combination of rage and hurt." He glanced at me again. "You shouldn't ever consider being a spy or a mole. You'd give everything away the moment anybody said anything to make you feel mad, glad, hurt or whatever. By the way, where do you want to be dropped? We're about to get to your house."

"Oh! Here's fine. Thanks." I wondered if he was going to ask where I was going to go from here. But he didn't. What made me say it I don't know, but I heard myself asking, "If you wanted to find out about somebody who'd lived here a long time ago, where would you go to find out?"

"Well—" He thought for a minute. "Depends how long ago you're talking about. If it was a hundred or so years ago, then I guess I'd see if the town had a historical society. If it was just a short while ago, I'd go to the local rag—the newspaper. It's a weekly. I'd look up back issues for whatever time I was interested in."

I hadn't even thought about that. "That's a terrific idea. Thanks." I hesitated. "Please don't . . . please don't, well, tell anybody what I asked about the newspaper, or about what I said about Ingrid."

"I won't," he said.

Especially Linda, I said silently as I got out, but I knew I couldn't say it out loud. "Thanks, Steve."

"De nada."

I stood there and watched his car go past our cottage and then turn right, following the line of the lake, and drive out of sight. Then I glanced at my watch. It was lunchtime, and ordinarily I'd be ravenous. But I knew that I had to face Daddy and his anger about my running into traffic the way I did, or running away at all. And then there'd be his questions about Elissa—that is, if she hadn't told him about the house in the woods. I thought about that for a moment, and somehow was sure she wouldn't have. But he'd probably want to know why I hadn't told him I was going to go riding, and how much would it cost?

And there was Morgan.

I wondered why I hadn't thought about him before. Normally I would be worrying myself into a stew. So why wasn't I?

Because he had gone sailing with Daddy. I'd have sworn he wouldn't have. Because I thought he hated it. But I was wrong, so maybe he and Daddy now had a sort of special all-male relationship.

"That's dumb," I said aloud. But it didn't feel dumb. Anyway, there was something I wanted to do before I did anything else. "Wanted" was almost too weak a word. I felt I *had* to.

Getting to the house took surprisingly little time. I went straight into the woods, then turned left and followed the way as though it were marked. A few minutes later I was there.

I went upstairs to the desk. I now had a name I wanted to find. I glanced quickly over all the letters that were already out both on the flap and on the table under Elissa's jacket. But once you know a name and can look for it, I could tell that whatever else I couldn't read, the two names, Patrick Bingham, were not there.

I then pulled out from the cubbyholes all the other letters, feeling the dry, almost powdery texture of the rotting paper in my hands. Again, with names to look for, it went much faster.

In about an hour, I found what I was searching for, smudged and blurred, but readable. In the upper left

117

corner of a letter was the name and address: Patrick Bingham, The Pines, RFD 2, Box 134, Jefferson, N.H. This time the shiver went all over my body.

—13—

"Patrick Bingham," I said aloud. And then again. "Patrick Bingham."

I don't know what I expected. The two names didn't make the walls shake or anything. Maybe I was hoping for some kind of mental flash of lightning. But nothing like that happened. After a while I decided I might as well go through the rest of the letters to see if I could find anything interesting or revealing.

It was a long, dusty, dirty job. The papers were smeared and blurred and pieces of them were missing. All I could get out of them involved someone named either Judy or Jennie or Jeanie who had gone somewhere, and one or two mentions of a baby. Also the word "drinking" seemed to crop up once or twice in the letters I managed to make any sense of. The whole thing seemed like it took hours. When I had gone through as many as I could, I had an awful headache and wanted more than anything to lie down.

I knew—or I was afraid that—if I went to sleep I'd have more of those awful dreams. I didn't want that, but as I sat and stared at the crumbling, faded paper, the desire to lie down was so strong I knew I couldn't fight it. I tried desperately to make myself think about the fact that I hadn't had any lunch, which was probably making me sleepier, that I didn't know what was happening to Morgan, that Daddy would be furious at me when I got back. But none of it was enough to stop me from pushing back my chair and going over to the sofa and lying down. I lay there for a few minutes, staring at the ceiling, at the stains on what must have once been a sort of creamy-colored paint. Brown stains, right above the desk. One stain was the shape of Australia. Another looked vaguely like a rabbit. The brownest part was literally over the desk. It must have been a leak, I thought muzzily, which was probably why the letters were blurred. But how would the leak get into the desk drawer? I was still trying to puzzle this out when I went to sleep.

I was again in that blue, blue water, swimming happily, and, in my dream, wondering how that turquoise water could have turned into brown stains. Then the voices came, a woman's, gentle and sweet, singing, which for some reason made me cry.

"Mamma," I cried. "Mamma!" The funny thing was, I knew it was a dream, even while I was dreaming.

And then, as before, everything changed and what changed it were the angry voices. First there was the man's voice, yelling, and the sound of things being thrown about, and then the woman's, not as nice as when she was singing. And then angry, like his. "Patrick!" she cried and then yelled, "Patrick!"

Then I couldn't hear anything for a while because they were yelling. In the midst of yelling there was crying. After a while I knew it came from a child. After another while I had just realized it was me crying when something started pushing me around.

"Bridget! Bridget! Wake up. It's Elissa. Wake up!"

"No, no, no," I cried. "No, no, no!"

" 'No, no!' about what?" Elissa asked. She was kneeling next to the sofa, shaking me.

"They were fighting," I said. I was partly in the

dream. Elissa was there, but the voices, raised, angry, were also still there. I could almost hear them. Then I sat up, and they went.

"Who? Who was fighting?" Elissa asked.

"Patrick and his wife."

"How do you know it was Patrick and his wife? The name was put into your head this morning by that man in the records place. You could have been dreaming because of that."

"I know," I said, and realized I was crying.

Elissa just sat there. I went on crying awhile and then started remembering when I'd last seen her.

I poked around in my pockets and found the handkerchief Steve had lent me. I blew my nose and wiped my eyes and managed to stop. "What happened, after . . . after I left?" I asked.

" 'Left' is a mild description of what you did. You ran straight into traffic."

"I wasn't hurt!"

"No. There was nobody left on the street when the cars finally stopped. You could, of course, have been hurt and gone on running. That's what was driving your father nearly crazy as he looked all over for you. I tried to tell him that if you had been seriously injured you couldn't have disappeared so completely. It wasn't true, of course, but I thought I ought to be as reassuring as I could."

"Oh." I stared down at the handkerchief. "Was he really worried?"

"That's one way of putting it! I don't know him, of course, and have no basis of comparison, but I've never really seen a parent as frantic as he was."

"Oh," I said again.

"Bridget, I think I know what drove you to do that insane thing. You were afraid he was going to start in on your—well, his concept that you're a little over-weight."

"His concept!" I almost yelled. "Everybody's—except, well, until this morning, yours. At least you never mentioned it to me." I paused, then looked up at her. "I suppose you thought it, anyway."

"Thought what?"

"That I'm overweight and gross and no man will ever look at me, et cetera, et cetera, et cetera!"

"If you want to know what I thought, I thought you were a chubby teenager who'd probably lose her weight as she lengthened out a bit, like thousands of other teen-agers who have a weight problem during their early teens and then lose it. It certainly didn't strike me as the most important thing about you."

"Daddy thinks it is, and of course Ingrid never lets me alone about it." I thought a moment, then asked, "Did you meet Ingrid?"

"Yes, when your father and I went back to your house."

"You went back with him?"

"Not in the same car, of course. In my own, but he wanted me to come there for lunch, and since I'd already incurred his wrath by letting you ride without checking with him first, I thought I'd better do it. For the farm's sake as well as yours."

"I'm sorry," I said drearily. Just as I thought, I decided; she'd now joined the enemy.

"Don't you think you'd better go and talk to your father?"

"I suppose."

"He's waiting for you, downstairs."

"He's here?"

"Yes. I just barely managed to keep him from coming upstairs."

I swung my legs off the bed. "Ingrid, too, I suppose."

"No. He and Morgan and I came."

"Morgan and Daddy now seem to be big buddies. Ever since Morgan went sailing with him."

"I can't comment, because I haven't known how he was with your father before."

"They weren't such great friends. Daddy's never been patient with him. He thinks that if nothing is wrong with him physically, then why can't he speak?"

Elissa got up. "Even in the brief while I've known him I'd say your father is not the soul of tact. It doesn't mean he doesn't love you. It just means he doesn't know how the things he says to you and to Morgan come across."

"Before the sail, Morgan would have been up here wanting to know if I was all right."

"He was forcibly prevented from coming up by your father. I said I wanted a minute to talk to you alone."

"Oh." I sat up straight. "Now Daddy knows about us coming here."

"Obviously. I had to tell him, Bridget."

"You could have said I met you through the farm."

"But it wouldn't have been true, would it? And in view of his worry, I thought he deserved to know the truth."

"I guess that's the end of my coming here—now that he knows." But even as I said it I knew that I'd manage to return even if he tied me to my bed and locked me in. I was shocked by how strongly I felt that.

"Bridget, I think I can understand your tendency always to forecast the worst possible scenario. But why don't you trust a little!"

"Why should I?"

"Probably because it will make you feel less sorry for yourself."

"That's a horrible thing to say! Well, it just shows I was right about that. Once you met him and Ingrid you'd stop being my friend!"

Elissa looked at me steadily. "No, you're not right about that. Now go down and talk to him. Please!"

I went slowly down the stairs, aware of the squeak of each rickety step and wondering how it sounded to Daddy. Would it make him all the more determined not to let me come back?

Daddy and Morgan were standing by the cobwebby fireplace. Daddy was staring at the cat, who was washing one of her kittens. The others seemed to be asleep. At the squeaks he looked up.

I stopped. "Hi," I said.

Morgan darted forward and up the stairs to me.

"Hi, Morgan," I said.

He flung his arms around my waist and I held him. "It's okay," I said, and rubbed his head. Then I put my arm around his shoulders and we went down the rest of the way together.

Daddy's face looked angry. "I can't imagine why you and Morgan have been coming out here. It's filthy, it's a ruin and it's probably overrun with rats."

"I think Tiger keeps them at bay," Elissa said, coming down the stairs behind me.

Daddy glanced at her, then back at me. "Why didn't you at least tell me you were coming here?"

"Because you would have said I couldn't, and if you hadn't at first then Ingrid would have made you."

"Ingrid doesn't tell me what to do."

"No, but the things she does say make you act the way she wants you to."

He frowned. "And why in God's name did you run out into traffic that way this morning? Elissa—Miss

Hamilton—said you were convinced I was going to comment on your weight problem.''

''You were, Daddy.''

''Well, as your father I should be concerned about your health, and that is certainly about your health.''

''It makes me feel gross and unattractive.''

''Well, if you don't—''

''Mr. Moorland,'' Elissa interrupted from behind me. ''I don't think the logical approach is going to get either of you anywhere.''

''Well, I'm sorry if you don't think much of logic, but if Bridget goes on the way she's going—''

''I mean,'' Elissa said, ''I think it would bring better—er—results, understanding between the two of you, if you thought more about how Bridget feels when you harp on her weight than about the logic of what you're saying.''

''I don't mean to hurt her feelings, but I'm trying to see that others won't.''

''Do you love her?'' Elissa asked abruptly.

I could hear him take in his breath. ''Of course I love her! That's a—an insulting question.''

''No it isn't,'' I said. ''I don't feel like you do. All this year I've thought you don't love me the way you do the twins and you're sorry you and Mother adopted me.'' And I started to cry again.

''I can't tell you how much I hate—hate this emotional approach. It's blackmail. Like saying 'If you say something I don't like then I know you don't love me.' Sometimes when you love somebody you have to say tough things!''

''But it doesn't work if the person you're talking to doesn't think you love her in the first place,'' Elissa said.

Daddy swung around. ''I wish I knew what your role in all this is. Ever since she got to know you—''

"No!" I yelled. "No! You're trying to blame it on her. I suppose you want her to be like that rotten Ingrid. Even Steve says every time she says something and you go along I look hurt and angry. I like Elissa. She doesn't think the only thing about me that's important is my weight."

"Considering how helpful Ingrid has been, I think you're very ungrateful. She suggested this morning, when you were riding, without my permission"—he turned and glared at Elissa—"that it might be helpful for you to go to a health farm for teenagers she knows of. You could spend the rest of the summer there and—"

"No, no, no, no!" It was Morgan, screaming words. Then he beat his fists against Daddy's front. "I hate you, I hate you, I hate you!"

"Morgan!" I shouted. "You talked!"

Daddy's face flushed. He leaned down and hugged Morgan. "So you can talk! That's wonderful, Morgan. That's great!"

"And there's also the content of what he said," Elissa said dryly.

"Look," Daddy said. "It'll only be for the summer. And you and I—What's the matter?"

Morgan's face had gone bright red, then his eyes filled and he started to cry, stuttering as he did.

I went over. "Morgan, Morgan, that's terrific. Can you say anything else? Like my name, maybe?"

Morgan, his face streaming, looked up at me. "B-B-Bridget."

"That's right," I said. "Exactly right." And I hugged him.

"Don't go." I couldn't believe that he said the words, but he did. They sounded funny, but I understood them. "Don't go. Don't go."

Daddy was staring at him. "We can't be selfish about something that is for Bridget's own good!"

"My what?" I said. "And who decides that, anyway?"

Daddy looked up at me. "I'm your father and as long as you're my daughter living at home it's up to me—"

"No I'm not. And I want to know something. Was my name Bingham? I mean my real name, the name of my real father!"

—14—

Even in the half light of the room I could see that Daddy had gone pale. "Who told you that?"

"It doesn't matter. Was it?"

"Bridget, listen—" Elissa began.

But I was too angry to listen or to care. "Was it Bingham?"

"If you must know, yes." He almost shouted it.

I let out a huge sigh and sat down on one of the chairs. My head was swimming. I felt dizzy and sick and excited all at once.

"I suppose you've been trying to find out," Daddy said. "Like a lot of other adopted children."

"Well, not at first—"

Daddy turned to Elissa. "Have you been helping her with this?"

She paused, then she said, "I have two answers to that. Would you please listen to both?"

Daddy nodded. I watched her.

"Answer one: Bridget and Morgan came in one day a few weeks ago. . . ." She paused. "Bridget got a sort of . . . well, a feeling from the house, as though she might have been here before; at least, that's the way I came to interpret it. And then, when she went upstairs she found letters in the desk with the name Patrick Bingham—"

I interrupted. "And I asked Elissa if she'd go with me to where the town records are kept, so we went there and found out the name of the man who owned this house and it was Patrick Bingham. After that I came back and went to sleep and dreamed about Patrick Bingham having awful fights with his wife, and I heard in my dream a child crying and I knew it was me."

"And on that evidence—that nonsense—you base your assumption that Patrick Bingham was your father—"

"But you just said he was!"

"You said you'd listen to the second part of my answer," Elissa said.

Daddy's mouth tightened. "All right," he said finally.

"According to present law," Elissa said gently, "Bridget hasn't done anything illegal. She has a right to find out."

"Legally, yes. But since you obviously approve of all this and have been aiding and abetting her, let me ask you a question. Do you think it was morally right or considerate without telling me?"

Elissa paused. "Perhaps not. But why don't you ask Bridget how she's felt this summer and what made her want to know who her real parents were?"

He turned to me. "Well, Bridget?"

"You never tell me I'm good at anything; you're always paying attention to the twins. You didn't ask me if I wanted to come up here and what I would do. You listen to Ingrid all the time who tells you I'm too fat. How do you think that makes me feel? Like a monster! You say it's for my own good. What good? You think the twins are great. But you've been different to Morgan because he couldn't talk. You've been different to me because I'm adopted. So naturally I want to find out who I was born to. Maybe it's not my fault I'm fat. I
129

read in the paper once it's inherited, mostly. Maybe my real parents were fat. Did you know them?''

''You want to know what I know? All right—''

''Mr. Moorland—''

''Oh no. You've been directing things in my family so far; now you can listen!''

''Please!'' Elissa said.

He turned to me. ''You want to know who your real father was? Well, I'll tell you! He was a drunken murderer who was sent to prison—'' He stopped. ''I didn't mean to put it that way, but after you've gone behind my back—''

''What do you mean, a drunken murderer?''

I could feel Morgan's hands pulling at my arms. He kept saying something like ''myfo, myfo.'' I finally realized he was trying to say ''My fault.''

''What do you mean?''

''I'm sorry,'' Morgan said haltingly.

''Listen to me,'' Elissa said. She knelt down so her face was near Morgan's. ''It's not your fault, Morgan. You didn't do anything wrong. It's wonderful you're talking. Just wonderful. You must keep on talking!''

''What are you talking about?'' Daddy said.

Elissa looked at him. ''If Morgan's muteness came from some psychological trauma, then it meant that unconsciously he was afraid to talk. Something terrible would happen if he talked. And something has!''

Daddy stared at both of us. ''Oh my God!'' he said, and walked across the room to the window. ''Oh my God!''

I felt nothing at all, which was very strange. Then I started to laugh. It suddenly struck me as wildly funny that after all the trouble of finding out who my real father was, I finally learned he was a drunken murderer.

''I should have known something like that. Why else would they put me up for adoption?''

130

Daddy turned. "Bridget!" He started to walk towards me.

"No!" I screamed. "No!" And I ran out of the house.

I didn't look where I was going. I just ran, dodging through the trees here and there until finally I found myself out by the main road. So I started to walk towards the town, because there was nowhere else to run.

I'd been walking for a while when I heard a car behind me. I was pretty sure it would be Daddy, and I made up my mind that I wouldn't get in, even if he tried to drag me in.

But it wasn't. It was Elissa. She opened the door.

"Get in, Bridget."

"No." I was angry at her, too. I was angry at everybody. Except maybe Morgan.

"You want to know more about Patrick Bingham and his wife. I knew them slightly."

That stopped me, as she knew it would. I got in the car.

When we drove off I said, "What were they like? When did you know them?"

"I knew them because both came occasionally to the farm to ride. That was when I was at art school and was here only sporadically. What were they like? Well, you look a little like your mother. You have her dark hair and blue eyes. Your father was tall and lanky and sort of dark blonde. When he was not drinking, he was pretty quiet. I never saw him when he'd been drinking, but according to local accounts, he became expansive and then angry. I don't know why your mother left your father; maybe because of the drinking. Anyway, she did. Unfortunately, she died, I think in a car accident, not long after. From what I heard, your father went to pieces, took up drinking in a serious way and must have lost his job and his house in Connecticut. Anyway, he came up here to live year-round in the house they'd taken for the summers. Then one night in a bar he got mad at someone and killed him. He was tried and sent to prison."

"Is he still there?"

"I don't know. If you really want to know as much about it as you can, then I'd suggest you go to the local newspaper and look up the papers of that time."

"How did Daddy—I mean my adopted father, and mother, of course—come to adopt me?"

"I don't know. Why don't you wait until your father calms down and ask him?"

"He wouldn't tell me!"

"He might."

I asked suddenly, "Was his wife Catherine Bingham?"

She glanced sideways at me. "Yes. How did you know?"

"I found a book with her name in it—*The Wind in the Willows*. It was wonderful!" So it was my mother's! Somehow I had known it.

We drove along for a while. Then Elissa asked, "What are you planning to do?"

I hadn't really thought. "Maybe go to the newspaper office."

"Aren't you hungry?"

"Yes." Unbelievably, I had forgotten about it until this moment. "I'm starved!" I said and got depressed. A real heroine in a book would have lost her appetite.

We stopped in the mall and Elissa parked. "What would you like to eat?"

All I could think about was a piece of pizza.

"A pizza," I said.

"A pizza it is," she said and got out.

We didn't say much while we ate, and it turned out I wasn't as hungry as I'd thought I was. I put the slice of pizza down half finished. "Even my real mother didn't want me that much, not if she left."

"You don't know the reasons, Bridget. That's why getting piecemeal information isn't a good idea. Don't judge either of your natural parents until you know the story."

I didn't say anything for a while, and then burst out, "A drunken murderer!" I started to cry. We were in a booth, so people didn't turn around, not that I would have cared.

"Finish your pizza and let's go to the newspaper office. There's no use in your sitting here and getting gloomier by the minute."

When the check was handed to us I sniffed and said, "I forgot to tell you, I don't have any money."

"Luckily, I do."

"Thanks."

When we got to the newspaper office Elissa turned to me. "This is your idea. You ask."

"What do you have on Patrick Bingham?" I asked.

The man went over to a desk and looked in a card file. After a minute he said, "The one who was tried for murder?"

"Yes."

He went away and then came back with a huge book, the size of a newspaper, only thick.

"You'll find a lot about it in here."

"Any particular date?" Elissa asked.

"Try March of that year."

Two hours later I closed the book. My head was in a whirl and I didn't know what to think.

What stood out were pictures of my real father being

taken into court in handcuffs, and my real mother, looking so much like me it was eerie, with an announcement about her death in a car accident only a few days after she'd left. According to a friend of hers who was interviewed when she was killed, she left me with my father only because he told her that if she tried to take me with her, he'd kill us both.

After that my father lost his job and his house in Connecticut and moved into the house in the woods, which he and my real mother had bought as a summer vacation place. According to various people the paper interviewed he'd go to a bar every afternoon when I was asleep and pick up liquor on the way home. One day in the bar, some guy made a comment about Mother and my father hit him as hard as he could. The guy struck his head when he fell and was killed. My father was tried on manslaughter charges and sentenced to seven years in jail.

Which meant that he was out now. Where would he be?

I glanced through the rest of the huge book, but there was nothing about my father or mother. I turned it in and went outside to the mall where I'd agreed to meet Elissa.

"Are you coming in with me?" I asked her when she drew the car up outside our cottage.
"No. I don't think I can do you any good, and you're going to have to face your father alone sooner or later." She hesitated. "I know you're not in a mood to believe this, but he does love you—in his fashion, which sounds derogatory, but I don't mean it that way."

"That's what Mother used to say. Why is it okay for him to love me in his fashion, whatever that means? But it's not okay for me to be me in my fashion. I mean, he's always telling me I'm not good enough."

"Parents are supposed to help their children grow up the right way, doing the things that will be best for them. I'm not a parent, but don't you think it might be hard to know when correcting somebody's the right thing to do, and when it's just nagging? Haven't you ever thought, when you read about some kid in the news doing something awful, why didn't somebody bring him or her up right?"

It was true. I had. "Thanks," I said, and opened the door and got out.

They were all inside, just sitting around. When I came in they stared at me.

"Where have you been?" Ingrid began.

"It's all right, Ingrid," Daddy said. He got out of his chair. "Why don't you and I take a stroll down the beach," he said to me.

"Okay." I didn't look forward to it, but it'd be better there than in the living room.

When we were down by the water Daddy said, "I'm sorry I spoke to you in that way back at that house." He paused. "I'm also sorrier than I can say that I've given you the impression that I regret that we adopted you. It's true, it was your mother who was the moving spirit behind that, but once I saw you and you became ours, I don't think I've ever thought of your not being ours, any more than I have of the twins or Morgan."

"But you like the twins. You think they're great."

He sighed. "Obviously I've given you no reason to believe it, but I think you're great, too." He paused. "Your mother was good at putting herself in other people's shoes. Somehow she always knew how they felt. I don't. Or I guess I don't try hard enough to." He turned and started walking towards the trees and I went along. "She once told me that if she and I were asked to investigate why a plant or factory's process wasn't work-

135

ing, I'd look at the structure—who first got the material, whatever it was, and who would it go to next—and I'd assume that that structure would have to be changed—that instead of A getting it first and handing it on to B, then C would have to get it first and hand it back to B. Do you see what I mean?"

"I guess so."

"Whereas if she had to find out what went wrong, she'd take all the people who handled the thing out to lunch one by one and find out how they felt about it and about what they were doing."

We walked along for a while.

After a minute Daddy said, "I'm sorry I called Patrick Bingham—your . . . your natural father—a drunken murderer. But he was an alcoholic and he did kill somebody."

"I know. I've just been reading the papers for that time. There's something I'd like to ask you."

"What?"

"Do you know when he got out of jail and what happened to him?"

"No. When we signed the adoption papers, I gave up any interest I had in him."

"Could you find out?"

"Is it that important to you?"

"Yes. It is."

We walked in silence for a while. Then, "All right," he said. He sounded unhappy. But I didn't care.

—15—

Morgan was talking more and more, although still not a lot. And when he did he wasn't always easy to understand. But he was getting better.

He and I went to the house in the woods in the mornings, and nobody tried to stop us. In fact, Ingrid hardly opened her mouth. One day Liza said, "Could we go to that house with you? It sounds creepy and wonderful."

"Did Daddy tell you about it?"

"Well, not exactly, but we heard him tell Ingrid."

"All right, but not now."

I didn't want them tramping all over the house which was my real father's. It was mine, or at least Morgan's and Elissa's and mine. The twins had the boat and the other people and Daddy. When I thought that, I realized that no matter how much he said he loved me, I didn't really believe him.

One day, when we were at the house, I picked up some of Morgan's drawings. A few of them were of the cat and the kittens. Most of them were brightly colored and had figures that were obviously people in them. They were really good. "That's Daddy," I said to him, "isn't it?" pointing at a figure that was standing in the front of a boat.

He nodded.

"You should take drawing and painting when you go to school this fall," Elissa said. She was often there in the morning, too, although her foot was a lot better and she was doing more and more on the farm.

"Yes," Morgan said.

In the afternoons we often rode. I'd ride in the ring for a while with Elissa coaching me. "No, Bridget, use your leg, not the rein. Remember how sensitive Belinda's mouth is! Think how it would feel if someone were pulling on your mouth!"

"Animals are nicer than people, aren't they?" I said.

She didn't answer right away. Then, "I think that, too, a lot of the time. But it's not a good thing to write people off. And remember, one reason why we like animals is because for the most part we can control them. But we can't control people and they can't control us." She grinned a little. "With people it's always negotiating time."

The following week Daddy said, "Let's take a little walk, Bridget. I have something to tell you."

I knew it was about my real father, and I was excited.

"What is it?" I asked when we were down by the lake.

"I made investigations about your . . . your natural father. You know the reason we adopted you was because the lawyer who defended your father was also our lawyer, and when your—Patrick Bingham had to go to jail, the lawyer, who knew your mother was interested in adopting a child, asked us if we'd like to adopt you. Both your natural parents were only children with no close relatives, so it was us or have the state put you in a foster home. So we adopted you."

"Did my—did Patrick Bingham want that?"

"Yes. Remember, I told you he was an alcoholic. He was in no great shape. He had no money for the bail, so by the time of the trial he'd been in prison and was suffering badly from withdrawal. Anyway, he was sentenced to two years to twelve, and he didn't really have much choice. He signed whatever papers the lawyer gave him."

I thought how awful it had been for him, how he'd been forced to give up his child—me. "How long did he spend in jail?"

"About four years. He was a good prisoner, went to AA meetings there, got counseling."

"Where is he now?"

"Out in Wyoming on a ranch. He went west when he got out, landed up there, went to work on a ranch, and was finally able to buy a small one of his own. He's also married again."

That was sort of a shock. But after all, why shouldn't he be? I was wondering how soon I could earn enough money to go out and see him when Daddy said, "I called him up a few days ago and asked if he'd like to see you. He said he'd be delighted. I didn't want to do this, but your friend, Elissa Hamilton, made me realize how . . . well, isolated and unappreciated you felt, so this is by way of making it up to you. If you want to go out for two weeks before school begins, I'll send you."

"You will!" I yelled and realized as I did that as well as being unbearably excited I was also disappointed. What I really wanted to do was earn the money on my own and go out in the face of Daddy's disapproval. But I said, "Thank you. Thanks a lot!"

When I told Elissa the next morning she said, "That's great!" She looked at me. "Your father's being very good about this, you know. Lots of adoptive fathers wouldn't be."

But I didn't really want to hear that. "I wonder what's going to happen to Morgan when I'm away."

"Morgan is going to take painting lessons and then go on riding in the afternoon."

"Who's going to teach him?"

Elissa smiled. "I am."

The last week before I left was strange. It was like I didn't belong to the family anymore. The twins seemed rather subdued. Ingrid stopped talking about how I ought to watch my diet.

Then one day she said something like, "After I've left—"

"You mean after *I've* left?" I asked. "After I've gone to Wyoming?"

"No. I mean me." And then she became like the old Ingrid. "You always assume everything refers to you, don't you?"

"Well, since I *am* going away, I don't think my question was so strange!"

She shrugged.

"Where are you going?" I asked.

She turned on a big smile. "I'm going to be married."

It was a terrific surprise. After a moment I said, "Congratulations." And managed not to add, And sympathies to your husband. But maybe she caught what I was thinking, because she suddenly went bright red.

"Where are you going to live when you marry?"

"Back home in Minnesota."

"I wonder what Daddy will do about the twins and Morgan."

"I'm sure he has other plans."

Somehow, I didn't want to know. Not even about Morgan.

I stayed very close to Morgan that last week. I knew he knew I was going and was unhappy about it.

"Morgan," I said once, when we were on our way to the house in the woods, "you're going to be fine. You're talking now, and things will be easier."

"Aren't you coming back?" he blurted out, and in the way he used to do, he tugged my hand.

"Of course." But as I said it, I knew I wasn't thinking I would. I'd be with my real father, who would love me and approve of me because I was his daughter. Everything would be different.

Daddy took me to the airport. I was to catch a plane to Boston and from there to Wyoming, and I had to promise him I'd call him the moment I was met.

I was so excited during the trip I could barely eat the food that was served. When I landed in a third plane in Jackson, Wyoming, I was tired, but didn't know it because I was so keyed up.

I got out of the small plane, and started to walk towards the little airport terminal. A tall man came through a gate towards me. He looked like a cowboy, I thought, with his broad-brimmed hat, but he didn't wear cowboy boots. Then he was standing in front of me. "Hello, Bridget," he said.

"Hi!" And suddenly I didn't know what to call him. "I don't know what to call you."

"Try Patrick. That's my name. Let's get your bags."

I had envisioned the scene so many times. He'd sweep me up in his arms and tell me he'd spent the last twelve years longing for his little girl. Instead, he simply said, let's get your bags.

We got into his car which was parked behind the terminal and he took off his hat. There was a little dark yellow in his hair, but it was mostly gray.

"Let's look at you," he said. And then he smiled, the skin at the corners of his gray eyes crinkling up. "You look like your mother, Bridget."

"Do you think I'm pretty?" The words fell out of me.

"Yes, and you'll be even prettier when you grow up. Is that important to you?"

141

"Ingrid—everybody thinks I'm too fat."

He started the car. "What's important is what you think of yourself."

It wasn't a new thought. Other people had said something like that. But I didn't know what to do with it. "Well, how can I think about myself different from the way other people do? Daddy's always talking about how I ought to lose weight."

"Maybe he's doing it for your own good. Ever think of that?"

It was like being punched in the nose. I thought he'd take me in his arms and tell me I was beautiful. "I thought you'd think I was beautiful!"

He started the car up. "I do, because you're my daughter, but that's not what I'd call an objective viewpoint. Your mother—" He stopped.

"My mother what?"

"Well, she was beautiful; everybody told her that. Much good it did her."

"What do you mean?"

"She had half the town in love with her and what did she do? She married a drunk who couldn't give her a decent life for herself and her daughter, so she ran away with one of the other men who admired her, who also drank and who was driving the car when they were killed in an accident." He turned and looked at me. "Being beautiful didn't help her choose good men or a good life, although half the girls in town who were jealous of her thought it did."

If Daddy had said that I would have been furious and decided he was just being mean. Now—I didn't know how I felt. Strange, tired, let down.

"I'm eager for you to meet my wife, Joanna." He turned the car out of the parking lot and headed down the road. "She's not what you'd call conventionally beautiful, but she's the most wonderful person I've ever met." Suddenly he reached out his hand and grabbed mine. Then he nodded to the side. "Ever seen mountains like those?"

For all the attention I'd paid, we could have been driving down a city street, but now I looked. The mountains rose, no foothills, no nothing, just straight out of the ground. I stopped thinking about what Patrick had just said and gasped. They were the most gorgeous and dramatic things I had ever seen. "They're beautiful!" I said.

He smiled then, and his face looked warm. "Yes, they are."

The fields curved away, with pine trees going up slopes on the other side. Cattle and horses grazed everywhere. "Are those hills the Tetons, too?" I asked.

"No, the ones on that side are the Wind Rivers and the ones a little back of us are the Gros Ventres."

"What a funny name."

"They were discovered by French mountain men. Gros Ventres means Big Stomachs. And they do look like fat stomachs."

I looked at them, at the rounded flattish tops. "Yeah, they do."

When we drove up to a low wooden house a door opened and a woman came out. She was dressed in jeans and a plaid shirt. She was quite tall and not thin, with a big nose and wide-apart dark eyes. She was not beautiful, but I knew exactly what Patrick meant. There was something terrific about her.

"Hi," she said, and smiled. "Come in. How was the flight?"

"Fine," I said and got out of the car. As we walked into what looked like a kitchen a girl of about six bounded through another door. "This is Rebecca," the woman said.

"Hi, Rebecca," I said to my half sister.

"And I'm Joanna."

I smiled. "Hello."

Patrick came into the kitchen behind me. "Meet everybody?" he asked.

"Yes."

"Dinner's in a couple of hours," Joanna said, "but maybe you'd like a snack."

It was weird, but I didn't want one. "Thanks, I'm not too hungry."

"All right. Why don't you go get yourself unpacked. Pat, why don't you show her where she's going to sleep."

I'd assumed it would be in the house, but he smiled and said, "You're going to get a cabin to yourself. Usually at this time of year it'd be occupied with guests, but the ones who were here had to leave suddenly for a family emergency back east so we thought you could have it. That way you wouldn't feel like you were falling over us. Do you ride?"

"Yes. I mean, a little. I rode for the first time back in New Hampshire, at . . . at Elissa Hamilton's horse farm." I looked at my father when I said that, wondering if he'd recognize her name.

"How is Elissa?" he said. "She spent most of her time at art school, as I remember."

"Yes. She paints beautifully. But she helps her mother with the horse farm now." I hesitated. I wanted to tell him the role she played in helping me find out who I was, but he was talking to Joanna.

"I'm going to talk to Stu about the mare," he said, picking up his hat from the side table. He smiled at me. "See you at dinner." He hesitated, took off his hat and then put it back. "Glad you could make it. I think it was real nice of your father to send you."

—16—

It was a strange, not to say weird, two weeks.

Ever since I'd known about my real father I'd imagined us having long walks, talking about everything, discovering how much alike we felt, how the worst part about his going to jail was that it meant giving me up and how finding me was the most wonderful thing that had ever happened to him. (Of course, a mean, buried little voice in me pointed out that he hadn't found me at all. I had found him. But I ignored it.)

Anyway, it wasn't like that at all. It's true he was nice. He took me riding when he took the other guests out. I learned about the western saddle, as well as the English, because they had both. He said once or twice that it was great for us to know each other again. But, when there were questions I wanted to ask and things I wanted to talk about, he wasn't around.

"Where's Patrick?" I said one morning when I got up late and came into the kitchen and dining room after almost everybody had gone. Joanna was putting some dishes in the dishwasher.

"He went to meet some guests from New York, so he ought to be back soon."

I stared out the window at a group on horseback

setting off on a trail. "Is this what they call a dude ranch?"

Joanna grinned. "Sort of. You were telling us about your friend's horse farm. Well, here it's not that different except people stay for a week or so and it's called a dude ranch. We have horses and people come, mostly in summer, and spend whatever time they're here riding."

I picked up a cup from the drainboard and poured myself some coffee. "What do you do in winter?"

"In winter we also have guests—some of the same guests—who ski."

"I somehow thought it would be the kind of ranch where, well, you had cattle."

"That's a very expensive operation. This way, as long as we have good horses and the guests are happy and keep coming back and sending their friends, we stay even."

"When did Patrick buy this?"

"He didn't, exactly. I inherited it from my father and Patrick came here to work after . . . after he came west."

"After he got out of prison."

"Yes."

"He never says a word to me about that, or about my mother or about how he feels about what happened. Whenever I think maybe we're going to get a chance for a real talk he has to do something else." I looked at her. "I'm beginning to think he doesn't want to."

She was flipping eggs over in the pan. "Get your plate, Bridget. These eggs are about done."

I said, sort of kidding, "What about my cholesterol?"

She looked at me above the pan, spatula poised. "Out here we don't have cholesterol."

I laughed. And I realized it was the first time I'd done

146

so since I'd been there. At that moment Rebecca, in her small, baggy jeans and large hat and cowboy boots came in holding a brown and white puppy. "Look what Daddy gave me," she said.

Joanna turned. "Rebecca! Where did he get it?"

"The Johnsons' dog had her puppies a few weeks ago. I wanted it and he said he'd give it to me."

Joanna looked down at her and then at me, and then down at her again. "All right, but you're going to have to train it, Rebecca."

"What's 'train'?"

"It means, Rebecca darling, if it pees on the floor or does you know what, you're going to have to clean it up."

"Oh." She looked down at the puppy, then placed a large smacking kiss on its head between its ears. "You're not going to pee on the floor, are you?"

The puppy wagged its stumpy tail. "You see, it says it won't."

The door opened again and in came Patrick with a couple dressed in tailored clothes.

"Joanna, these are the Penwrights. I'll take them to their cabin, but I thought they might want some coffee or something to eat."

"Of course." Joanna held out her hand. "Good to see you. Now sit down at the table there and I'll be happy to pour you some coffee and cook some eggs. Bridget here is about to have hers. Bridget is my step-daughter."

It made me jump. I'd never thought of Joanna as a stepmother. "Hi," I said.

The man said, "I don't suppose you'd have anything as decadent as a drink. It was a long flight and a long wait between connecting planes."

"Sorry." Patrick spoke more abruptly than I'd heard him. "We have no objection to guests bringing their own bottles and fixing their drinks before dinner, but Joanna and I don't have any."

"All right. Wish you'd told me sooner; I'd have stopped off in the town to get some. I don't suppose you could get me any if you're going in there. After all, we don't have a car. Or I could drive with you and buy some."

"Okay," Patrick said. "You can go into town with me this afternoon and get some if you want."

There was a small silence. He didn't offer to buy the man a bottle, I noticed, and I was pretty sure the guests did, too. I suddenly remembered Daddy's words, "He's a drunken murderer," and I shivered a little.

"Sit down, Bridget," Joanna said. "Or your eggs will be chickens."

The Penwrights collected their cabin key and left with Patrick, having turned down any food. When they'd gone I said, "Patrick doesn't drink at all, does he?"

"He joined AA in prison and he still doesn't like to have any around, although we have to allow people to have drinks from their own bottles if they want to."

"Don't you have anything to drink, either?" I thought about Daddy back in New Hampshire always having a drink before dinner. I'd only once seen him have two and that was when his guests did. But most of the people we knew had drinks.

"No. I'm in AA, too; that's where we met. A lot of people who've had problems with alcohol are not crazy about having it around, and your—and Patrick had a particularly terrible time, as you know. The memory of having killed a man when he was drunk is with him most of the time."

I sat there eating my eggs. When Daddy told me about Patrick having committed the murder it was a

148

horrible shock, but after that I thought mostly about his being my father, and wouldn't anybody drink if his wife ran off with somebody else? My real mother not only abandoned me, she abandoned my real father.

"Well, his wife, my real mother, left him. I guess it's natural he drank."

Joanna put down her spatula and turned the fire out under the frying pan. "Bridget, I love your father very much and he is a wonderful person, but I don't think you ought to find excuses for him. He doesn't for himself. Staying sober very much depends on his seeing things as they were. Your mother left him because when he drank he beat her. And she left you only because he threatened to kill you, too, and she felt she had to get help for you both. Unfortunately, she was killed before she could. Your father went crazy when he drank. It does that to some people."

I sat staring at my second egg and realized tears were coming down my face.

Suddenly I felt her hand on my shoulder. "I didn't say that to hurt you. I said it to help Patrick. He mustn't forget what happened. His sobriety, his sanity depends on that." She patted my shoulder and then held me close to her. "If you want to cry, go ahead. I know none of this has been easy for you."

At that moment Patrick opened the door and came in.

"Penwright seems to want to go to town to buy that bottle right now. I sure hope it doesn't mean he's going to get drunk every night." He took a cup off the drainboard and poured a little coffee into it.

"I hope not, too," Joanna said, putting the frying pan into the sink.

"You don't like people to get drunk around you?" I asked, looking at Patrick.

"No. I don't. I've seen enough boozy people to last the rest of my life and I don't want to have them lurching around the dining room and cabins."

"Do you miss it?" I asked. "I mean, do you hate not drinking?"

"No, I don't miss it, and no, I don't hate not drinking, but once an alcoholic, always an alcoholic, and don't think that in moments of stress the old siren song doesn't play again."

"Did Mother drink?"

He looked at me. "Sure she drank. Whether or not she drank alcoholically I can't remember. I was too drunk myself most of the time. But it's something you ought to think about."

"Why? Da—my adoptive parents don't drink much."

"Because it's now known that alcoholism has a strong genetic element. This came from tests on children of alcoholic parents brought up by nonalcoholic adoptive parents."

"Thanks a lot," I said, and heard my sarcasm. I had meant to say it jokingly, but it didn't come out that way, maybe because I wasn't feeling particularly jokey this morning.

"Sorry about that." Patrick put down the cup and went to the door.

"Can I go with you—into town, I mean?"

"Sure. I'll be waiting out in the car."

"Do you think he's mad because I said that?" I asked Joanna.

"No. But talking about alcohol—outside an AA meeting, that is—often makes him uncomfortable. It shouldn't, of course, but he had a pretty rough story."

I sat in the back while Patrick drove and Mr. Penwright sat beside him. The Tetons, like a row of giants, lined the road.

"How tall is the tallest of the mountains?" I asked.

"About thirteen thousand feet," Patrick said.

"Is that as high as Mount Everest?" I wasn't sure why, but I wanted to keep Patrick talking with me.

He laughed. "Not exactly. I think Mount Everest is around twenty-eight thousand. Something like that."

"How much would I have to divide that by to make it into miles?"

"Dunno. What would you say, Penwright?"

"I haven't the faintest idea—or interest. What I do have is a king-size headache."

"Sorry," Patrick said. "We'll keep quiet." I saw him look at me in the rearview mirror. I smiled into the mirror, but he didn't smile back. His eyes shifted to the road.

We got into the town and parked in front of a liquor store. "Okay," Patrick said. "Go on in there. Bridget and I'll wait for you."

Mr. Penwright moved fast, getting out of the car and going into the liquor store.

"Do you think he's an alcoholic?"

"I try never to diagnose somebody else. But there's not much doubt about his anxiety when his supply is cut off."

"Maybe you could take him to an AA meeting."

"Only if he asks me to."

There was a silence that grew.

Then Mr. Penwright came out, smiling and carrying a bag. He got into the car. "Sorry, everybody, if I was a little terse. Let me invite you all to a drink. There must be a bar around here somewhere."

"Thanks, but no," Patrick said. "I have work to get back to, and Bridget is too young by nearly a decade."

"Not that young," I said, angry.

151

Mr. Penwright winked at me. "We'll wait until he's out of the way, won't we?"

"I'm sure you're joking," Patrick said. "But as I said, and meant, Bridget is too young."

We drove back in silence. Mr. Penwright got out of the car and went towards his cabin.

"Bridget, I want you to stay out of his way. You asked me if I thought he was an alcoholic. The answer now is, yes. He couldn't wait to get back to his cabin but must have taken a large swig while he was still in the liquor store. I wish to God he weren't here. Well, if he starts misbehaving in any way while having drinks before dinner, then I'm going to ask him to go."

"What are you going to do now?" I asked.

"I have stuff to do in the barn."

"Couldn't we take a walk, or maybe go riding together?"

"Bridget, I'd like to, but I can't just take off when I feel like it. We have a ranch to run and guests to serve and that has to come first. Maybe later." And he got out of the car and started to walk off.

But he didn't get very far. Rebecca suddenly appeared on the steps of the ranch house. "Daddy," she called. "Come play with me."

He turned and went over to her, picked her up and held her. "I can't now, sweetheart. I have to go and do some work."

"Please. Just a little. Put me up on Rosebud so I can ride. She hasn't gone out, has she?"

"No. All right! All right! You're too persuasive for me. Let's go and find Rosebud."

I stood there while he put her down. She took his hand and they went off to the barn.

Joanna stepped through the open door onto the step. "Don't be upset, Bridget."

152

"She's his daughter, not me. That's pretty obvious."

"I know it looks that way. I also know it must be harder for you than anyone can imagine. I don't know what to say."

"He doesn't care about me, does he?"

"Yes, he does. And I can tell you absolutely truly that he talks about you a lot. The trouble is, you're part of a past of which he is bitterly ashamed, and Rebecca is part of the present that has redeemed him."

I went slowly into the kitchen. The puppy was in the middle of the floor making funny whimpering noises. Joanna was on the phone in the small study off the dining room.

"Well, Puppy," I said. "We've both been left." I bent down and stroked its head. A warm tongue licked my hand. The puppy wagged its tail and then squatted and peed on the floor.

Joanna came back in. She sighed. "I knew this would happen. And I suppose Rebecca's off somewhere with Patrick and Rosebud."

"Yes."

She went over to the sink and tore off several sheets of paper toweling. "I could shake Patrick. Rebecca's too young to understand what training a puppy means. But of course Patrick didn't think of that."

She came over to the puddle.

"I'll do that," I heard myself say. I took the paper from her and, squatting down, cleaned up the puddle. "It's not that bad."

"No. Not a simple little pee like that. Wait until he does something a lot messier. To say nothing of diarrhea, which most puppies and kittens seem to have at some point. Well, it goes outside." She started to bend down.

"No!" I said suddenly. "I'll train it. Let me."

"Have you ever trained a puppy?"

"No." I picked the puppy up and held it and looked at it and felt my face being enthusiastically licked. But I have to remember it's Rebecca's, I thought.

"You have to confine it to a corner of a room and cover that corner with paper, so that when it does something it will always do it on paper. If it gets out and does something elsewhere, then you have to tap it gently but firmly with a folded newspaper. Otherwise you'll end up with a grown, untrained dog. And dogs like that frequently end up pushed outside or given to the pound where they're unadoptable and destroyed within a few days."

"That's awful!"

"Yes, it is. Which is why I want to take it back to the Johnsons. I cannot possibly do it at the height of the summer with all the guests here, and Rebecca's too young to be expected to stick with the discipline of training it. When she's eight or nine I'll get her another one."

"You're going to take it back?"

"Yes. Their chances of finding a new home for it are much better now, when it's young and appealing, than later."

She took her handbag from the counter. "You can come with me and hold it if you want to."

"Now?"

"Yes, now. I want to get rid of it before Rebecca has had a chance to get really attached."

"What will Patrick say?"

"Patrick's responsibility is the horses and the barn and taking guests out. He can't stick around the ranch house for several months to train a puppy. And he wouldn't want to. Now pick up the puppy and come along. I'll drive us to the Johnsons' before I have to fix lunch."

I held the warm puppy against my chest as I followed

154

her out. But when she went around the car to the driver's side I said suddenly, "I'll train it. And I'll take it back east with me."

"What will your father—your adoptive father—say?"

"I don't know. But I don't want the puppy to be abandoned. I know how that feels. Anyway, it's not a he, it's a she."

We stood there for a moment.

"All right. It's yours. But please keep it in your cabin. I don't want Rebecca to be more distressed than necessary. Sometimes it's hard to be the parent who plays the bad cop."

At that moment I felt a warm trickle down my ribs and waist. I jerked the puppy away and looked down.

"Welcome to parenthood," Joanna said.

"I'd better get her back to my cabin," I said. "Where can I find some newspaper?"

"I'll bring you some, and I'll also bring a portable fence that I used when Rebecca was a baby. And give me your shirt and jeans and underpants, if they're also wet. I'll shove them in the washing machine."

When she came to the cabin with the papers and fence I had on fresh jeans and a T-shirt, and was sitting with the puppy, who was on the floor, sound asleep.

"Here." She handed me the papers. "I think that corner there would be good for the fence, and I've brought a sort of bed for her to lie in."

We arranged everything and put the sleeping puppy in the low box lined with toweling and an old sweater.

"I guess you don't want this sweater anymore," I said.

"No. It's full of holes and I'm about to knit myself another."

"What do puppies eat?"

"At that young age, some kind of puppy chow. I'll drive you into town after lunch and we can get some." She paused, then said, "Your father—your adoptive father—called this morning. He's going to drive out here to get you and should arrive on Tuesday."

—17—

I decided to name the puppy Abby, for Abigail, a very girl-type name. Joanna's occasional helper, Maggie, had turned up, so Joanna and I went to town to buy Abby's puppy chow before lunch. We had returned and I was asking her how much and how often to feed Abby when Rebecca, back from her ride with Patrick and Rosebud, ran in.

"Where's the puppy?" she demanded.

Joanna went over to her and put her hands on her shoulders. "Honey, I think the puppy is too young for you. You know I said you'd have to train her? Well, that's an awful lot of work even for a grown-up. If you want a pet, I—your father and I—will get you an older dog, one that's already trained, or maybe a half-grown kitten. Cats aren't anywhere near as much trouble to train as a dog."

Rebecca stared for a few seconds. Then her face seemed to break into a variety of pieces and she started to howl. "I want my puppy! Daddy bought her for me. I want my puppy!"

Quietly I slid the bag of puppy chow behind the door into the dining room. At that moment Patrick came in. "I want you to know that Rebecca rides on Rosebud like she was twelve years old! No fear, no nothing!"

Rebecca ran over to him and clutched his arms, tears

pouring down her cheeks. "Mom took away my puppy. She says I'm too young! I want my puppy!"

"Rebecca—" Joanna began.

"You did what?" Patrick said, staring at Joanna. The lines on his face that I hadn't noticed before seemed to be drawn in black. "I gave her that puppy. You had no right to do anything with it. What the hell do you mean, she's too young?"

"Patrick," Joanna said, "can we talk about this some other place?" Her voice was quiet, but her face had lost its color. She looked older.

"What's to talk about? I give my daughter something she wants and you take it away—"

"Patrick, let's at least go outside. Rebecca's too young to take full responsibility for cleaning up after an unhousebroken puppy."

"So what if it does make a few messes? Can't we all pitch in and help clean up after it?"

"When, Patrick? When? You're going to stay home from the trails?"

"Okay, so you take over when I'm not here. I don't see why you should object to that just to give the child a little pleasure."

"Have you ever trained a puppy?"

"I don't see what that's got to do with it!"

"It's got everything to do with it, and I'm going to tell you right now I'm not going to spend my time hurrying around a kitchen and risking stepping into one slithery mess after another. I have trained dogs, and I know what I'm talking about. And how confident will you be if guests get sick and claim that food was contaminated because I was supposed to stop and clean up after a puppy when I was preparing their meals? How do you feel about getting sued?"

"You had no right—" It was like a tape recorder, going over and over.

"Stop it!" I screamed. "Stop it! Rebecca, you want your puppy back. Fine, take it. I know my own father wouldn't be giving me anything for myself!" And I ran over to my own cabin, snatched up Abby, who gave a yelp, and ran back. "Here," I said, thrusting the puppy into Rebecca's arms. "She's yours!"

Maybe it was just a coincidence, maybe the puppy was upset by all the goings on and being snatched up, but she chose that moment to loose a lot of watery diarrhea down Rebecca's shirt and jeans.

"Oh, yuck! Pi-ew! You stink!" Rebecca squealed and threw the puppy from her. It landed on the floor yelping painfully.

I went over and stroked it.

"Here," Joanna said, handing me some wet paper toweling. Then she went over to her daughter, who was staring with horror at her shirt and jeans. "All right, Rebecca, let me get some of this off. Then take off your shirt and jeans and I'll soak them."

Carefully I wiped Abby off. Then I took her outside and put her down. She ran around for a bit, then started whimpering. So I picked her up, wondering if she would have a second bout with the runs. But she cuddled into my arms.

Patrick suddenly emerged from the house. "I'm sorry I gave you the impression I wouldn't ever give you anything. Joanna—Joanna has persuaded me that if your father will let you take the puppy back, it's better for you to have it." He spoke stiffly. "I'm sorry," he said again. And then walked off to the barn.

Tuesday, when, according to Joanna, Daddy was supposed to show up, was four days off, and I spent a lot of the time with Abby. She was a sweet puppy, and had plenty of energy to play. I bought some toys the next time somebody drove to town and made others. I man-

159

aged to ride at least once a day, usually with a group led by one of the other wranglers, not Patrick. This wasn't because he didn't from time to time ask me. But I was pretty sure he was doing it because he thought he ought to, or Joanna told him he should, and I always found an excuse for not going out then.

Then one day he appeared at the cabin door and said, "Why don't we take a ride and have that talk you've been talking about?"

"I didn't think you wanted to."

"To tell the truth, you're right. I didn't. But—"

"But Joanna says you ought to," I said, and knew I shouldn't have.

"No, *mirabile dictu*, I thought of it all by myself."

"What does mira—whatever it is—mean? Is it Latin?"

"Yes, it's Latin, and it means 'marvelous to relate.' Who'd ever think now that I was once a newspaper reporter with ambitions to be a writer?"

"When I was looking in the house in the woods—the one that the man in the records department said you and Mother took for the summer and then you lived in with me before . . . before—"

"Before I screwed things up even more by killing somebody. There's no point in tiptoeing around the fact. I killed a man, I went to jail and I deserved every bit of it. It took me a long time and a lot of AA to admit that. But the second thing they told me, after 'Don't pick up a drink one day at a time,' was that I was responsible for what had happened to me and to accept that fact." He paused and watched me holding a ball on a string for Abby. "You were saying that when you were looking in the house in the woods—what? What were you going to say before I interrupted you?"

"I found a lot of papers in the desk. Some were letters, and it was in one of those that I found your name after learning it in the records office. But a lot of the

160

writing wasn't letters, at least I don't think so. I couldn't read most of it. There was a stain in the ceiling right over the desk, so some water may have leaked on it or mice had eaten it or something. Anyway, were you writing a book then?''

"Probably. My memory of those last months isn't too sharp. But that's what I likely thought I was doing, recording for posterity my sad story and all the injustices I'd had to bear!'' There was an edge to his sarcasm.

I put the puppy behind the fence, made sure she couldn't get out and then said, "Okay, let's go for the ride.''

He put me on a horse named Japhet and swung his leg over his own. "I thought we could go up near that pass where we can see Idaho,'' he said. "I ought to take another look at that trail.''

We rode in silence for a while. Now that we were out together I didn't know where to begin. I stared at the rolling green fields and the mountains behind and sniffed the sharp air that had a tang of pine in it.

"You asked me once what your mother was like,'' Patrick said finally, "and I gave you the smart-aleck answer that I couldn't remember. Well, that's not entirely true. I can't recall much of our last year together, except, as you know by now, there was a lot of violence on my part. But you remind me of what she looked like when we married. I met her when I was in journalism school in New York. She was in her first year when I was in my third, and when I was offered a job as a reporter on my hometown paper in Connecticut, I persuaded her to quit so we could get married and go back there. My master plan was that I would put in a few years on a small paper and then be ready to accept the many offers I'd be getting from the major newspapers—the *New York Times*, the *Washington Post*, the *Wall Street Journal*.

161

"Unfortunately, my drinking, which was already well under way, intervened. I messed up some opportunities, felt, of course, that I'd been unjustly blamed by the boss, and drank more.

"Your mother and I bought that house in the woods for the summers, and then you arrived. I was not what you might call ready for the responsibilities of fatherhood. My drinking increased. I got fired, couldn't meet the mortgage payments on the main house in Connecticut, and, as I said and as you know, started . . . started acting violently.

"Your mother left to get help but died in that car crash before she could. I took you and one elderly maid who'd been with the family up to New Hampshire. You know the rest."

"I'm sorry," was all I could think of to say. I could hear the pain behind the sarcasm.

"It—God knows—is not your fault. I've been one lousy father. I thought the kindest thing I could do was give you up for adoption to the Moorlands, whom Jack Taylor, my lawyer, said wanted you. I'm sorry if it turned out I was wrong."

"No. You weren't wrong. They've been good. Mother died, of course. And Daddy—well, I've always thought he preferred the twins, who are thin and like doing what he likes, like sailing. Of course there was Morgan. Daddy's never been good with him. He's always thought that if there was nothing wrong with him physically, then the fact that he couldn't talk was . . . well, sort of his imagination or that he was being stubborn."

"He sounds like a practical man, not very good on sensitivity and/or empathy. I must say you haven't had much luck with fathers. Or maybe—now, don't get mad—you expect too much. People who don't have much self-confidence always want the world around

162

them to reassure them all the time. I know what I'm talking about, Bridget, because I'm like that myself.''

"Maybe I get it from you.''

"I wouldn't be surprised. Which makes me say something I'm afraid you won't like. What I just described is a very alcoholic trait. Maybe the disease itself has missed you, but maybe it hasn't.''

"How will I know?''

"I guess by finding it out. But if it turns out you can't drink normally—that you don't know when enough is enough, or once you've started you can't stop—then I hope to God you find it out before I did.'' We rode for a while. "You said something about your father, your adoptive father, preferring the twins because they're thin. Your mother had that obsession. She showed me pictures of herself during her teens and you look exactly like her. But apparently she got thinner without too much grief when she was around sixteen or seventeen, and to my knowledge—although I grant I wasn't up to much noticing during those last years—she didn't have any further trouble with it.''

At that moment his horse stumbled a little. He tightened the rein. "Take it easy, Mopsy.'' Then he put his horse up a low hill through some trees and I followed him. When we were up and going along a ridge he said, "Bridget, blind as I am even I have observed that you think you're unattractive. Take it from me, you're not. You're a pretty girl, and when you get a little older, you'll probably be stunning. But that's not really what a guy will want you for—at least not on a permanent basis.'' He leaned across suddenly and tapped me gently in the middle of my chest and on my head. "It's what's there and there that counts.''

Others had said the same, or similar, but I'd always thought it was just adult double-talk, especially when the person who said it had another time made a big thing of my going on a diet, because having a good figure was the most important thing about me. But now, Patrick's words somehow sank in. I felt a slight pricking behind my eyes.

When we got back and put the horses back in the barn he leaned over and kissed me on the cheek. "Your parents—your adoptive parents—have done a wonderful job. And I want you to have a good life," he said.

Playing with Abby somehow made me think of Morgan. I wondered how he had been getting on. After he had started talking I assumed everything would be all right. Now I found myself worrying about him again. I wondered about his painting, which made me think about Elissa and the house in the woods.

One evening when we were getting ready for dinner I said suddenly to Patrick, "Are you going to sell the house in the woods?"

"I should. I guess I've been postponing it because I was afraid to find out if I owed taxes on it or anything. Not very responsible, I'm afraid." He looked at me a moment. "If you were a bit older, I'd say it's yours. But if there is any money due on it, I don't see why you should be saddled with it. Why don't I write to your father and see if he or we can work out some reasonable deal on it, so it's yours to do with as you want, but you're not going to be owing the state or the township any money."

"Yes," I said. "Thanks." I liked the idea of the house being mine. Maybe all it really needed was cleaning up, but then I thought about the leaky ceiling and knew that wasn't entirely true.

Then it was Tuesday. I woke up early and found I was excited. What Patrick had said, "You haven't had much luck with fathers," rolled around in my head. I guess

I'd expected too much. That thought brought me down a bit.

"Did Daddy say what time he was coming?" I asked Joanna at breakfast.

"No, but somehow I assumed he meant late afternoon."

"Okay."

I went back to the cabin with some food for Abby, then took her out in front of the cabin where she obediently did her business. "Good girl," I said, "very good girl," and gave her a small treat, just like the keepers in the zoo at home with the sea lions or the lion tamers in a circus.

A car drove slowly up the path, looking like any of the many cars that had come since I'd got here. Then two figures got out and when they came towards me I realized who they were.

"Daddy!" I screamed. "Morgan!"

"Bridget!"

They both ran. I couldn't believe how excited and happy I felt.

Daddy got to me first. I felt his arms go around me and he was hugging me tight. "I'm so glad to see you," he said. "I can't tell you how glad!"

"Bridget, Bridget!" Morgan said, then flung himself at the two of us and put his arms around us.

"Oh, Daddy, I'm glad to see you, too!" I said, not believing how much I felt it.

He held me away for a moment. "You are? Truly?"

"Yes," I said. "Truly!" And I hugged him. I knew it was true, and that I was glad to be going home.

About the Author

Isabelle Holland, the daughter of an American diplomatic officer, was born in Basel, Switzerland. After living in several countries, she moved to the United States to finish college. She spent a number of years in publishing before turning to writing as a career. In addition to her numerous young adult books, Ms. Holland writes about mysteries. She lives in New York City.